He'd got exactly what he wanted.

For weeks he'd been trying to deny the attraction between him and Tess, focusing his efforts on courting her and trying not to think about the night they'd made love. His proposal might have been motivated by a desire to give his baby a family, but now that they were married, he found himself wanting more.

And right now he wanted Tess in his bed.

She'd finally agreed to marry him so that their baby could have a full-time father. Their marriage was a means to an end. So why wasn't he happy?

Because he wanted *more*. He wanted it all.

He almost laughed out loud. He had a challenging and rewarding career, a beautiful home in the suburbs, a child on the way. What else was there?

Love.

Available in September 2008
from Mills & Boon®
Special Edition

The Rancher Next Door
by Cathy Gillen Thacker

The Marriage Solution
by Brenda Harlen

Her Best Man
by Crystal Green

The Baby Bind
by Nikki Benjamin

From the First Kiss
by Jessica Bird

Finding His Way Home
by Barbara Gale

The Marriage Solution

BRENDA HARLEN

MILLS & BOON
Pure reading pleasure™

First published in Great Britain 2008
by Harlequin Mills & Boon Limited,
Eton House, 18-24 Paradise Road, Richmond, Surrey TW9 1SR

ISBN: 978 0 263 86069 6

23-0908

Harlequin Mills & Boon policy is to use papers that are
natural, renewable and recyclable products and made from
wood grown in sustainable forests. The logging and
manufacturing processes conform to the legal environmental
regulations of the country of origin.

Printed and bound in Spain
by Litografia Rosés S.A., Barcelona

For Neill, the man I love
and who also happens to be my best friend.
And for Jamie, with thanks.

BRENDA HARLEN

grew up in a small town surrounded by books and
imaginary friends. Although she always dreamed
of being a writer, she chose to follow a more
traditional career path first. After two years of
practising as a lawyer (including an appearance
in front of the Supreme Court of Canada), she
gave up her "real" job to be a mum and to try
her hand at writing books. Three years, five
manuscripts and another baby later, she sold her
first book – an RWA Golden Heart Winner.

Brenda lives in Southern Ontario with her real-
life husband/hero, two heroes-in-training and two
neurotic dogs. She is still surrounded by books
("too many books," according to her children)
and imaginary friends, but she also enjoys
communicating with "real" people. Readers
can contact Brenda by e-mail at brendaharlen@
yahoo.com

Dear Reader,

I'm always amazed by the unexpected consequences that result from seemingly ordinary events. An example from my own life is when I met Jamie in university. We played baseball together, shared a couple of classes and then he invited me to a party. An ordinary event…

Five years later, I married a man I met at that party. Unexpected (and very happy) consequences…

Tess Lucas and Craig Richmond are two longtime friends trying to get their relationship back on track after spending the night together. But the events of that ordinary night (OK, it was better than ordinary – after all, Craig is the hero) have unexpected consequences.

Now Tess is pregnant and there are some serious decisions to be made. He wants to get married; she doesn't. At least they both agree on one thing: falling in love is NOT an option.

They are about to find out that sometimes the most unexpected and extraordinary things do happen.

I hope you enjoy their story.

Best,

Brenda Harlen

Chapter One

Craig Richmond tapped his foot impatiently as he waited for the door to open. He knew Tess was home—he'd called first to make sure, determined that her campaign of avoidance was about to come to an end. He wasn't going to let their fifteen-year friendship fall apart just because they'd made the mistake of sleeping together.

Not that *he* thought it was a mistake. More like a long-denied fantasy finally realized. But Tess obviously regretted making love with him. And while he was disappointed that there wouldn't be a repeat performance of their one night together, he wasn't going to abandon everything they meant to one another because of it. Tonight they were going to talk about what happened and find a way to move past it.

At last the door opened and she was there.

He drank in the sight of her, from the dark, slightly

tousled hair, wide eyes the color of a clear summer sky and temptingly full lips, moving lower, lingering a moment in appreciation of her feminine curves before following the endless length of shapely legs.

He'd been angry that she was ignoring his calls, hurt that she was shutting him out, but mostly he'd been lonely without his best friend. He'd missed her smile and her laughter, her warmth and compassion. He'd missed talking to her and just being with her. And because he'd missed her friendship so much, he was determined to ignore the desire that stirred whenever he was with her—as he'd ignored it for so many years already.

He met her gaze, saw the confusion and awkwardness he felt reflected in her eyes and forced a smile. "Hi."

"Hi," she replied to his greeting.

He waited for her to step back and invite him inside, but she remained on the threshold, barring his entry.

He shifted the takeout bag he carried from one hand to the other. "Can I come in?"

She hesitated a moment before she responded, "I told you on the phone that this isn't really a good time."

"There hasn't been a good time for the past several weeks," he pointed out. "And I'm not leaving until we've had a chance to talk. So we can talk here, in the hallway, or you can invite me in to share my Pad Thai."

"I'm not very hungry." But she finally stepped away from the door and let him in.

Craig went directly to the kitchen, as comfortable in her apartment as he was in his own, and took two plates from the cupboard. Tess hovered uncertainly behind him as he divided up the noodles. He glanced back at her, noted the pallor of her cheeks and the dark smudges under her eyes that had escaped his initial scrutiny. He wondered if memories of their lovemaking had been keeping her awake at night, too, and derived a certain amount of satisfaction from that thought.

"Let's eat," he said, carrying the plates to the table.

She sat across from him, eyed the meal warily.

He frowned at her obvious lack of interest, but determinedly dug into his food. Several minutes passed in silence while he ate and Tess poked at her noodles. Then he heard her fork clatter against the plate. He looked over and saw that her cheeks weren't just pale now, they were tinged with green.

"Tess—"

Before he could say anything else, she shoved back her chair and raced down the hall. He heard the slam of the bathroom door and the muted, yet unmistakable sound, of retching.

He pushed his own plate away, his own stomach feeling a little unsettled now, too. Maybe Tess had a touch of the flu that was going around.

Or maybe there was another explanation for both her physical symptoms and her determination to avoid him since the night they'd had sex and the condom broke. Maybe she was pregnant.

Tess Lucas stared at the pink cardboard box in Craig's hand and felt her cheeks flush the same color. Last night, he'd shown up at her apartment with dinner. Today, it was a pregnancy test.

She closed her eyes, as if that would make the box—and the possibility—go away.

She'd been feeling tired and nauseous for a couple

of weeks now, but had assumed she had probably caught some virus. And the tenderness in her breasts was likely an indication that she was about to get her period. Because she *was* going to get her period—any day now, she was sure. Then she could stop worrying about the possible repercussions of faulty latex.

Unfortunately, when she opened her eyes again the box—and Craig—were still there.

She took the package from his outstretched hand and moved into the living room, dropping it on the coffee table before sinking into her favorite overstuffed chair. Craig followed her into the room but remained standing.

"That isn't quite what I expected you to do with it," he said dryly.

"What did you expect?"

"That you'd be as anxious as I am to know the truth."

"The truth is that it's been a long week and I don't have the energy to jump to conclusions like you're doing." She'd been trying for casual, but the strain in her voice was obvious to her own ears.

"I'm not jumping to any conclusions yet," he responded in a tone that was infinitely patient and reasonable.

Of course, Craig was always patient and reasonable, calm and unflappable. It was one of reasons he was such an effective vice president at Richmond Pharmaceuticals, the family-owned company he would run someday.

Tess couldn't even fake that kind of control. She couldn't pretend that the possibility of pregnancy didn't terrify her. She wanted children—someday. But not now and not like this. She felt her stomach rising again and drew in a deep breath, trying to will the nausea away.

"Please, Tess. Take the test."

"Why are you doing this?" she asked wearily.

"Because I think it would be better to know for sure than to sit around worrying about it," he told her.

"Well, I don't." She didn't care if she sounded unreasonable to him. She didn't want to know the truth; she didn't want to think about how completely and irrevocably a baby would change her life.

"You need to find out," he said gently. "So that you can consider your options."

"I'm twenty-nine years old—I know what my options are. And *if* I'm pregnant, I'll have the baby." Although she strongly believed that a woman had the right to make her own decisions about her body, she had no doubt what hers would be.

Craig nodded toward the table, to the pregnancy test she'd tossed aside. "Why don't you take the test, then we'll know?"

As much as she hated to admit it, she knew he was right. He usually was. She grabbed the box and took it to the bathroom.

Her heart was pounding, her head was spinning and she felt as though she was going to throw up. Again.

She closed the door behind her and pried open the end of the box with trembling fingers. The contents spilled out onto the counter: one page of instructions and a foil-wrapped plastic stick. It certainly looked harmless enough, not like something that had the power to change her whole life.

And, of course, it didn't. Her life—or at least her relationship with Craig—had been changed by her own actions.

The attraction had been there from the beginning—

at least on Tess's part. A shy teenager, she'd developed an almost painful crush on him. But she'd kept her adolescent dreams locked deep inside and they'd become friends. Now almost fifteen years of friendship were in jeopardy because of one night of insanity.

Not that everything had changed in that one night. There had been subtle shifts in their relationship over the years—casual flirtations and occasional tensions. But they'd mostly managed to ignore those undercurrents for the sake of their friendship. Until the night they'd made love.

She'd hoped they might somehow manage to get past what had happened, but she wasn't optimistic. Not when the mere sight of his mouth brought back memories of his lips moving over her body and the most casual touch reminded her of his hands caressing her bare skin. How could they possibly resume any kind of platonic relationship when she couldn't forget that she'd been naked with him—and couldn't stop wanting to get naked with him again?

But right now the awkwardness between them was the least of her worries. More important, was deciding what she was going to do about her future. Because she didn't need the test to tell her the truth she'd been trying so hard to deny, that she'd known deep inside for almost two weeks now. And the truth was that the tiny being she carried in her womb—Craig's baby—had already taken firm hold of her heart.

But he would want the proof, so she peed on the stick and waited. And while she waited, her mind wandered and worried.

She didn't know what his thoughts and plans were

with respect to having a family—except that he'd recently broken up with the latest in a seemingly unending string of girlfriends because she'd been hinting about the future and he wasn't ready to commit to anything further than a week away. And while Tess had always dreamed of having children one day, she'd also hoped to have a husband—someone with whom to share the joys and responsibilities of raising children. After finding her fiancé in their bed with his ex-wife, she accepted that that was another dream that wouldn't be a reality. She would have this baby on her own and make whatever adjustments were necessary to her life to be the best single mother she could be.

She stared at her watch as the final seconds ticked away.

Then she took a deep breath, wiped her hands down the front of her skirt and picked up the plastic stick. According to the instructions, if there was only one line in the window, she wasn't pregnant; if there were two lines, she was.

She turned the stick over.

One.

Two.

Her knees suddenly buckled and she sank down onto the edge of the bathtub.

She was going to have a baby.

She was overwhelmed.

Terrified.

And just a little bit excited.

A baby.

Tess didn't know whether to laugh or cry, but she knew that nothing in her life would ever be the same.

* * *

How long did the damn test take?

It was the question that dogged his heels as Craig paced across the tile floor of Tess's kitchen.

There had been a whole shelf of pregnancy tests in the pharmacy and he'd read the directions on every single one, wanting to make an informed choice, to make this difficult process a little easier for both of them. As if anything could. But he was certain he'd at least picked the box that promised the quickest response.

Who knew that two minutes could seem like an eternity?

Or maybe Tess was still balking at taking the test. Maybe she wasn't ready to face the results.

He couldn't blame her for being scared. Since he'd first acknowledged the possibility that she might be pregnant with his child twenty-four hours earlier, he'd felt as though there was a vice gripping his chest— an increasing pressure that stole his breath at unexpected moments.

After the end of his brief and regrettable engagement more than a year and a half earlier, he'd been careful not to make any promises or commitments to the women he dated. He'd certainly never contemplated fathering a child with any of them. A baby was the ultimate responsibility—a lifelong commitment—and one that he had no intention of taking on. Ever.

He refused to bring an unwanted child into the world—refused to give any woman that kind of weapon to wield against him in battles about custody and access and child support. No way. He knew only too well what it was like to *be* that weapon and he'd decided the only way to ensure the same thing would never happen to any child of his own was to never have children.

So he'd always been careful about birth control, determined to protect any woman he was with as much as himself. And while he was aware that no method of contraception was one hundred percent effective, he'd never before had a condom break.

The fact that it had happened with Tess both relieved and frustrated him. He knew she didn't sleep around, so the only potential repercussion to worry about was pregnancy. But that was a huge worry, not just because he wasn't ready—and might never be ready—to be a father, but because he hated to think how an unplanned pregnancy would affect Tess's life. She was his friend, his confidante—the one woman who meant more to him than any other—and he'd failed to take care of her.

He winced at the selfishness of his own actions. He'd known immediately that something had happened, but he didn't pull out. It felt too good to be inside her, deep in the warm heat of her body. And then her legs had wrapped around him, her fingernails had dug into his shoulders and he'd been helpless to do anything but follow the urging of his body and drive them both to the finish.

He shoved his hands into his pockets as he continued to pace. The last thing he needed to be thinking about right now was making love with Tess, but as hard as he tried, he couldn't seem to banish the memories. And if he couldn't think about that night without guilt and remorse, he also couldn't forget how perfect everything had been up to that moment when he'd realized the condom had broke. He couldn't sleep without dreaming of her and then he'd wake and ache with desires.

He'd known having sex with her would change their friendship and he'd expected a certain amount of awkwardness. But he hadn't expected that he wouldn't be able to look at her without wanting to get her into his bed again.

He forced the tempting picture from his mind and glanced at his watch.

She *must* have finished the test by now.

The sound of her shoes clicking softly on the tile seconds before she stepped into view confirmed that she had.

Her eyes were wide, her cheeks white, her lips pressed tightly together.

Despite her obvious distress, he felt some of the pressure inside his chest ease. Maybe it was strange, but he'd found the not knowing worse than the truth. Now, at least they could face their future.

"We're going to have a baby," he said.

She nodded slowly.

He wanted to take her in his arms, to reassure her that they were in this together. But he suspected that she wouldn't appreciate the overture, especially since it was his desire to comfort her that had led to another kind of desire and landed them in this current predicament.

She moved past him into the kitchen and he caught a whiff of her scent, something subtly fruity and distinctly Tess. He felt the stir of desire again, immediately followed by a stab of guilt at the realization he was lusting after his best friend—the woman who was pregnant with his child.

She opened the fridge and pulled out a can of ginger ale. "Do you want one?"

"Sure," he agreed.

She passed him the can and took another out for herself, popped the top. Her hands, he noted, weren't quite steady and her complexion had taken on the slightly green tinge he recognized from last night's incident with the Pad Thai.

"Are you going to be sick?" he asked.

"I hope not." She took a long swallow of her soda. "But someone needs to fix this baby's internal clock because my supposed 'morning' sickness usually seems to strike in the evening."

"Has it been very bad?" he asked, both curious and concerned.

She shook her head. "I can't complain. I remember my sister was sick all day during the first few months of her pregnancy with Becca."

"I'm sorry, Tess."

"About what—the nausea or my pregnancy?"

"Both," he admitted.

"Don't be," she said. "Even though this wasn't planned, I want this baby."

"What can I do?"

Her smile was wry. "You've already done your part."

"As I recall, we did that part together."

"You're right." She dropped her gaze as her cheeks colored. While Tess had always been frustrated by her blushing, he'd always been fascinated by it. She was a smart, savvy professional woman, and yet the pinking of her cheeks hinted at an innocence that was surprisingly arousing and incredibly tempting.

"And we'll do the rest together," he said. "I'm not going to leave you to deal with this on your own."

"I am on my own and I can manage this pregnancy on my own."

He should have guessed that was how she'd approach this. Strong, capable, independent Tess—she didn't need anyone or anything. As she was constantly reminding him whenever he made the mistake of offering to help. Her independence was one of the things he admired about her even when it frustrated the hell out of him.

But this time, he wouldn't let her cut him out of the equation. It was, after all, his baby she was carrying and he was determined to find a solution that would work for all of them. "We could get married."

Tess stared at him, clearly stunned by his suggestion.

Okay, he was a little surprised, too. He didn't know where those words had come from, had no clue that such an idea would pop out of his mouth. But now that it had, he realized it was, in some ways, a logical response to the situation. A baby deserved to be loved and cared for by both parents, and marrying Tess would ensure that they'd both be involved in their child's life.

Since his close call with Lana, the mere thought of committing himself to any one woman for the rest of his life was enough to make him break out in hives. Yet here he was not just thinking it but saying it. Out loud.

He tugged at his tie, swallowed.

Tess seemed to recover from her shock first, because she laughed.

He frowned.

"I'm almost tempted to say 'yes'," she told him. "Just to see if your face could possibly get any whiter."

"Instinctive reaction to the M-word," he admitted.

She smiled gently. "I know."

"That's no reason to laugh off the suggestion." And now that he'd spoken the word out loud—without choking on it—he found the idea taking root in his mind.

"You're kidding, right?"

"We're going to have a baby. Why shouldn't we get married?"

"Is that a question or a proposal?" she asked. "Because if it's a question, I can give you a thousand reasons why we shouldn't get married. And if it's a proposal, the answer's no."

"A thousand reasons?" he challenged, both relieved and annoyed by her automatic refusal.

"Starting with the fact that you don't want to get married," she reminded him.

She was right. He could hardly deny it now when he'd told her exactly that when he'd broken up with Lana and repeated it numerous times since then.

The truth was, he loved women—blondes, brunettes, redheads. He loved the way they looked and the way they moved, their scents and their softness. He loved everything about them, but he'd never fallen *in* love with any of them.

Tess believed the scars from his mother's abandonment prevented him from opening his heart, and maybe there was something to that. When Charlene Richmond walked out of her husband's home she'd abandoned not just her marriage but her children. One day she was there and the next she was gone, and he'd been devastated.

She came back a few months later, claiming to want the sons she'd left behind, but Craig had already learned not to trust too easily or love too deeply.

"Maybe I've changed my mind about marriage," he said to Tess now.

She shook her head. "I need you to be my friend more than I need a husband, Craig."

"I am your friend." He took her hands in his, linked their fingers together. "That doesn't mean I can't be more."

"Anything more will only complicate the situation."

"It seems to me the situation is already complicated." She unlaced their hands and stepped away from him.

"You could at least give it some consideration," he said.

"No," she said again.

"You're being unreasonable, Tess."

She didn't think so. Unreasonable had been going home with Craig, kissing him, touching him, falling into bed with him. Now she was facing the consequences of those impulsive actions and she was determined to do so rationally and reasonably. She'd expected that he, of all people, would appreciate a logical approach to the situation. "I don't expect anything from you, Craig."

"Why the hell not?" he demanded.

She blinked at the anger in his tone. "Because…I'm not going to hold you responsible for something that was my fault."

"Do I have to remind you again that we made this baby together?"

"You know what I mean," she said, ignoring the heat that infused her cheeks. She certainly didn't need him to remind her of the night they'd made love—the night their baby had been conceived.

"No, I don't."

She sighed. "We both know that what happened that night only happened because you were feeling sorry for me."

He placed a finger under her chin, forced her to look at him. "Do you actually believe that?"

Uh-oh. This was dangerous. The simple touch set every nerve ending in her body on full alert and the way he was looking at her now had her hormones rocketing.

She'd often thought a woman would have to be blind not to notice his obvious good looks, and Tess's almost perfect vision allowed her to fully appreciate the sun-kissed golden highlights in his dark blond hair, the deep brown eyes fringed with gloriously long lashes, the wide, full mouth that quirked easily into a grin, and the strong, square chin that held just the hint of a dimple. Then there was the body: six feet four inches of lean, solid and dangerously sexy male.

She'd known Craig since she was in junior high— he'd been in high school, an assistant coach of her baseball team and a basketball player himself. His wiry body had filled out since then. His shoulders were broader now, his muscles firmer.

But Craig Richmond was a lot more than a terrific face and gorgeous body. There was an aura about him, a confidence bordering on arrogance and the sheer force of his personality drew her even as her common sense warned her to stay far away. And now, just the touch of his hand on her chin was enough to send her pulse racing.

She knew he was waiting for an answer, but she couldn't even remember the question. God help her, he'd simply touched her and her mind had gone blank.

"Do you really think I made love to you out of pity?" he asked.

She swallowed, her throat suddenly dry. "Didn't you?"

He smiled, a slow, sexy curving of his lips that caused her heart to trip over itself. "No."

The single word skimmed over her like a caress—teasing, tempting. She forced herself to pull away from him. She couldn't afford to let her hormones overrule her common sense, not again.

"We made love that night because it was what we both wanted," he reminded her.

She closed her eyes, trying to shut out the all too vivid memories. She didn't want to remember how incredible it had been, the way she'd responded to Craig's kisses, his touch. The way their bodies had come together, naturally, instinctively, as if they'd been made for each other. Even as she'd moved beneath him, she'd been painfully aware that no one had ever made her feel the way he did, and she knew that no one else ever would. Because no one else knew her like Craig did, no one understood her as he did. And the realization terrified her.

"I threw myself at you," Tess said miserably. "I was feeling rejected and alone. I needed someone that night and you were there."

His eyes narrowed. "Don't pretend it wasn't personal, because I don't believe that for a minute. The attraction has been building for a long time—since the kiss we shared under the mistletoe last Christmas, if not longer."

"That kiss didn't mean anything," she lied.

He propped a hip against the counter and quirked a brow. "Wanna try it now—so I can prove you wrong?"

"No," she responded quickly.

His lips curved.

She crossed the room, needing to put some distance

between them. This trek down memory lane wasn't doing any good and it certainly wasn't helping to solve her current dilemma.

"Friendship and chemistry are both solid foundations for a relationship," he said. "And if we got married, our baby would have a real family."

He almost sounded like he meant it—as if he *wanted* to marry her and be a father to their child. And though she wished, more than anything, that she could give her baby a family, she couldn't do it like this. Marrying Craig for all the wrong reasons wouldn't be right for any of them.

"It's the twenty-first century," she reminded him. "Our child won't be ostracized by society because his parents never married."

She couldn't believe they were even having this conversation. All this talk about marriage and family from a man who wouldn't date any woman for more than a month in case she got ideas about commitment, was making her head spin. Obviously her pregnancy had shaken both of them.

"Can we both just take a step back?" she suggested. "Let the reality sink in before we make any definite plans for the future?"

For a moment she thought he was going to refuse, but then he asked, "How far back?"

"I don't know. I know there are a lot of decisions to be made, but I need time." She looked up at him, silently pleading with him to understand. "I don't want to screw this up. I don't want to ruin our baby's life by making bad choices."

"You won't."

"How do you know?" she asked, her words less of a challenge than a plea for reassurance. "How am I supposed to know what's the right thing to do?"

"We'll figure it out together."

"I wasn't sure—after that night…"

"What?" he prompted gently.

She just shook her head.

"Why are you so determined to forget how spectacular we were together that night?"

She looked away from the heat in his eyes and tried to ignore the answering warmth that spread through her body. Spectacular didn't begin to describe the night she'd spent in his arms. "Because remembering won't do us any good."

"Don't you think physical compatibility is important in a marriage?"

"I think you should have your head examined."

"Why won't you at least consider it?" he challenged.

"Because I still have a dress hanging in my closet as a memento of the last man who promised to love me forever."

She saw the shadows pass over his face, like clouds blocking out the sun. "I won't make you any promises I can't keep," he said. "But I will take care of you and our baby and I will be faithful."

She felt as if her heart was breaking—not just because she wanted more than he was offering, but because he believed he wasn't capable of giving more. She had faith in the healing power of love, but Craig's statement proved that the scars left by his mother's abandonment still hadn't healed and she had to wonder if they ever would. And she refused to set herself up for heartbreak by marrying someone who couldn't love her.

"We made this baby together," he continued when she didn't respond. "And we should share that responsibility. Not just for the next eight months, but forever."

Then he kissed her lightly on the cheek and walked out.

Chapter Two

Two weeks later, after the shock had worn off and he'd had time to think, Craig kept circling back to the same place. Maybe marriage and a baby weren't a life-long dream of his, but he owed it to Tess—and their baby—to do the right thing. And as much as he racked his brain for another solution, he'd started to believe that marriage was the best one.

He wanted his baby to have a father and he wanted to help Tess, and marrying her would accomplish both of those objectives.

Which is exactly what he told her when he stopped by her office Friday afternoon.

"We should get married."

Tess turned around so quickly when he spoke that she knocked her coffee mug, spilling its contents all over the papers spread out on her desk. She swore under her breath as she moved her equipment out of the way of the spreading puddle.

As Craig hurried to the small kitchen to find a roll of paper towels, he realized he probably shouldn't have blurted it out the way he had.

His mother often teased that he had a way with words and a natural charm that could persuade anyone to do what he wanted. He'd thought Tess would appreciate a straightforward approach. The silence that stretched between them as they worked to clean up her desk caused him to question that assumption.

She didn't say anything at all until her wastebasket was filled with wet towels and illegible pages and the remaining papers had been spread out to dry.

"In the future, you might want to open a conversation with 'hello'," she suggested.

"Sorry," he said. Then he smiled. "Hello, Tess."

"Hello, Craig," she responded politely.

He dropped into the chair beside her desk. "Now that we've dealt with the social niceties, can we get to the reason I'm here?"

"Please," she agreed. "I'd like to know what's behind the sudden change in your attitude about marriage."

"The baby," he admitted. "Our baby needs a father."

She was quiet for a moment, considering his statement, then she nodded. "I don't disagree," she said. "But do you really want to be the baby's father—or do you just want to do what you've convinced yourself is the right thing?"

"I want to be a father." Parenthood wasn't something he'd ever looked forward to in the abstract sense, but now, knowing his best friend was pregnant with his child, he found it was true.

"I'm a little surprised," she admitted. "But I'm also relieved. I think our child will benefit from having both of his parents involved in his life."

"His?" he wondered aloud.

She shrugged. "I don't know yet, of course. But it doesn't seem right to refer to the baby as 'it'."

He could see her point and while he hadn't given much thought to the gender of their child, he found he liked the idea of having a son. A little boy who might grow up to take his place in the business Craig's grandfather had founded. Of course, a girl could do the same thing. And when he thought about it, he found himself intrigued by the idea of a daughter—a little angel who looked just like her mother.

"Whether the baby's a boy or a girl," he said. "I don't just want to be involved, I want to be there for him, or her, every day. I've been thinking about this since you took that test—I've hardly been able to think about anything else—and I really believe marriage is the perfect solution."

"I didn't ask you for a solution," she said.

He took a deep breath, tried to figure out what he'd said or done to put her back up. Because it was obvious to him now that her back was up about something.

"I'm only trying to help," he said.

"Just like you were helping when you took me home that night?"

She winced, and he knew she regretted the words as soon as she'd spoken, but that couldn't erase them. Nor could it alter the truth in them. She blamed him, as he blamed himself.

"I'm sorry," she said. "That was out of line."

"No," he denied. "You have every right to be mad at me. If I'd been thinking about what you needed instead of what I wanted, I would have just been your friend that night."

She managed a weak smile. "I think I was pretty clear on what I needed."

Yeah, she had been. But he should have looked beyond the invitation in her eyes, beyond the softness of her lips and the yield of her warm curves. Except that having Tess in his arms had been a dream come true and he hadn't wanted to let her go.

Her smile faded as she folded her hands on her desk and faced him solemnly. "I'm not angry with you," she said. "But maybe you should be angry with me."

"Why?"

"Because—" she hesitated, her teeth sinking into her bottom lip. "Because I'm not sure I didn't get pregnant on purpose."

He frowned. "What are you talking about?"

She looked down at the fingers laced together in front of her and took a deep breath. "You know how much I've always wanted a family of my own," she began. "Especially since my mom died. When I broke off my engagement to Roger, that dream seemed to slip away from me and that hurt more than anything else."

She swallowed. "I didn't set out to get pregnant. At least, I don't think I did. But I wonder if, subconsciously—"

"Tess," he interrupted gently. "The condom broke. It had nothing to do with your conscious or subconscious desire for a family."

She dropped her gaze again. "The condom broke because it was more than a year past its expiration date."

He stared at her, stunned, as the events of that night replayed in his mind.

He mentally fast-forwarded through all the hot, sweaty stuff to the relevant moment when he'd realized they were in the guest room and his condoms were across the hall in his bedroom. He'd intended to go to his room to get them, but Tess had surprised him by admitting there were some in her purse. Since her purse was on the dresser beside the bed—a helluva lot closer than the night table in his bedroom, which was at least thirty feet away—they'd used the ones in her purse.

The out-of-date condoms.

"I didn't know it at the time," she said quickly. "I didn't know until I checked the box when I got home."

"Why didn't you check the box before you bought them?"

Her cheeks colored. "I did. But I bought them a couple of years ago—when Roger and I first started dating. But he always took care of protection and I never really thought about it afterward."

"You've been carrying those condoms in your purse for two years?" he asked incredulously.

She shook her head. "I only opened the box a couple of months ago when I decided that I was going to prove to myself that I was over Roger. But I didn't have any need for them…until that night."

"Not until that night, huh?" He couldn't fight the smile that tugged at his lips.

Tess eyed him warily. "You're not mad?"

Maybe he should be angry, at least annoyed. But he

knew Tess, and he knew, despite her own concerns to the contrary, that she would never have gotten pregnant on purpose.

"Do you believe in fate?" he asked.

Her expression grew more wary. "I'm not sure."

"I'm not sure, either," he admitted. "But I can't help thinking that fate has been sticking her nose into things since you broke mine."

"That wasn't fate," she scoffed. "That was *you* staring at Barb MacIntyre instead of paying attention to the baseball game."

His smile widened. "I was fifteen and Barb MacIntyre had breasts."

Tess shook her head, but she was smiling now, too. "You should have been paying attention to the skinny kid with the bat."

"I'd never known a girl who could smack a line drive like that," he told her, wincing a little at the memory. But he'd sure as hell paid attention after that. Not just because he'd been impressed by Tess's athletic abilities, but because something in her wide blue eyes had tugged at him when she stood over him—as he'd lain bleeding all over the dirt at third base—and asked if he was going to die, too.

Several weeks later, he'd learned that was the same day she'd buried her mother—and been taken directly from the funeral to her new foster home. She was a fourteen-year-old orphan with more guts and attitude than he'd ever seen, but he recognized that the stubborn tilt of her chin and the angry glint in her eyes only masked the pain she carried inside. And he knew—even then—that she would wreak havoc on his life.

What he didn't know and couldn't have guessed, was that she'd also become the best friend he'd ever had.

He rubbed a finger over the bump on the bridge of his nose.

Tess's eyes followed the motion and the corners of her mouth twitched as she tried, not entirely successfully, to hold back a smile.

"You're not still mad about that, are you?" she teased.

He shook his head. "That broken nose was one of the best things that ever happened to me. I didn't think so at the time, of course," he confessed. "But in retrospect, I can appreciate that it's the reason we became friends."

"What does any of that have to do with now?"

"I think in another fifteen years we'll look back on this and realize your pregnancy was the best thing that could have happened."

"I already know it is," she confessed softly.

"Then why is it so hard for you to imagine that us getting married could be another one of those things?"

He didn't quite manage to disguise the impatience in his voice, and Tess sighed.

"It's not that I can't imagine it," she admitted.

In fact, it was almost too easy to picture herself married to Craig, sharing the joys and responsibilities of parenthood with him, building the family she'd always wanted with him.

But although her heart yearned for the whole fairy-tale package, she knew it could never exist outside of her dreams. Because he wasn't her Prince Charming and her pregnancy wasn't something they'd planned for or dreamed about together. As far as she knew, Craig didn't even want kids—it was just his deeply-ingrained sense of responsibility that refused to let him walk away from their baby.

"Then what is it?" he demanded.

She didn't know what to say, how to explain the battle that had been waging inside her since she'd seen those two lines on the stick. She could do what was easy—or she could do what was right. And she really wanted to do what was right.

The buzz of the intercom saved her from answering, at least for now.

"Carl's on line three," Elaine, the receptionist, announced.

Carl Bloom was one of the owners of SB Graphics and, therefore, one of Tess's bosses. Which meant she needed to get Craig out of her office and her mind back on the job.

"Thanks," Tess replied. Then to Craig, she said, "I have to take this call."

"I can wait," he said.

"I'd rather you didn't. This is probably going to take a while and I have a meeting with Owen Sanderson—" Carl's business partner and her other boss "—later this afternoon that I still need to prepare for."

"We need to finish this conversation," he said.

"I know," she agreed. "But not now."

"Then come to my place tonight for dinner."

She stared at the blinking light on her phone as she considered his invitation, the light flashing like a neon "danger" sign inside her head. But what was the danger in sharing a meal with a friend?

"Okay," she agreed. "I'll see you later for dinner."

"Seven o'clock," Craig said as he rose from his chair.

"I've got steaks we can barbecue—red meat has lots of iron, it'll be good for both you and the baby."

She shook her head as he walked out the door.

When she'd first suspected she might be pregnant, she'd worried about telling Craig. She'd tried to anticipate his reaction and had guessed that he would either balk at the idea of being a father and slowly but inexorably distance himself from her and the child she carried, or he would resign himself to the consequences of their actions and fulfill his responsibilities with respect to child support and weekly visitation. She hadn't expected him to embrace the idea of parenthood.

Then again, the idea might be easier for him to embrace than the reality. Once their child was born, he might change his mind about what he wanted.

Or he might not, she admitted on a sigh. And that was an even greater concern for Tess, because she'd never known Craig to give up on something he really wanted.

She pushed these disquieting thoughts aside and reached for the phone to talk to her boss.

The software program Tess was revising was being especially stubborn, and the last couple hours of fighting with it had caused her hands to cramp from too much keyboarding. She raised her arms over her head to stretch out the tight muscles and glanced at the clock above her desk, surprised to note that it was already quarter to seven. She was supposed to be at Craig's for dinner in fifteen minutes.

She saved the program, then shut down her computer and called to let him know she'd be there soon.

Making a quick trip to the ladies room, she wasn't surprised to find that all her coworkers had gone and the outer office was empty and dark. When she'd first graduated from DeVry University, she'd accepted a position at a huge software company in Arizona. She'd enjoyed her work there, but the hours had been long, her bosses demanding. She'd come back to Pinehurst even knowing that her chances of landing a job as a programmer were less than slim because she'd wanted to have a life outside of her work and because she'd wanted to be closer to her stepsister's family and Craig. She'd been thrilled—and very lucky—to find SB Graphics.

SBG was a digital animation software company which had been started almost twenty years earlier by Owen Sanderson and Carl Bloom, both MIT graduates. Although the partners had talked about moving the business to Los Angeles, they'd come to realize they could compete with the big corporations on the west coast from their location in Pinehurst.

They were both family men who not only appreciated that their employees had lives outside of the job but insisted upon it. In fact, when Deanna, one of the team leaders, had given birth to her first child last year, the bosses had encouraged her to take whatever time she needed at home with her baby. Then, when she'd made the decision to come back, they'd let her work from home or bring the baby into the office as required when day care was a problem.

Tess hadn't thought about it much at the time, but now that she was expecting a child of her own, it was a huge relief to know that her employers understood and were sympathetic to the demands of parenthood. She could only hope that the father-to-be would be as considerate and accommodating of her needs.

We should get married.

As if the words hadn't been surprising enough, the conviction with which he'd spoken them had completely unsettled her. She knew, probably better than anyone, how unyielding Craig could be once he'd made up his mind about something. For some reason, he'd decided marriage was what he wanted. Now she was going to have to convince him there were other alternatives.

She ran a brush through her hair then slipped into her blazer. Maybe if she looked like a together, professional woman she would feel like a together, professional woman when she and Craig discussed their baby's future. Maybe he would actually listen to her when she offered a more suitable—more reasonable—solution.

She sighed as she zipped her purse. Yeah, and maybe she'd go to bed tonight and wake up to find it was the day after her canceled wedding and she was alone in Craig's guest room because nothing had happened between them the night before. Except that she wouldn't really wish that night away even if she could. She might not be looking forward to doing battle with Craig about what was best for their baby, but she wanted this baby. More than anything, she wanted this baby because it meant she would never be alone again.

Her stomach growled, loudly protesting that it had been ignored since it rejected the chicken salad sandwich she'd had for lunch several hours earlier. As she made her way down the hall, her mouth watering in anticipation of the juicy steak Craig had promised her, she noticed the light on in Owen's office.

She knocked before peeking around the partially open door. "I was just on my— Oh," she halted her explanation when she realized Owen wasn't behind his desk and another man was in his office. "I'm sorry. I thought you were Mr. Sanderson."

"Jared McCabe," he said, rising to his feet and offering his hand.

"Tess Lucas," she told him, moving forward to take it and wondering, as she did so, why his name sounded familiar to her.

His gaze narrowed speculatively. "You were the team leader on version four of DirectorPlus."

DP4 was an easy-to-use software interface utilized by animation directors to control background characters in movies and video games. She nodded in response to his statement even as she wondered how he knew she'd worked on the project—and why she couldn't make such an easy connection with his name.

"It's a terrific program," he said.

"Are you a customer of SB Graphics?"

He smiled. "Potentially."

"Then you'll be interested to know that version five is going to be even better," she promised him.

"I'm counting on it."

His comment struck her as strange but before she could ask what he meant, Owen stepped into the room.

"Jared, I found—" He stopped in mid-sentence, obviously surprised to see her. "Tess, I didn't realize you were still here."

"I was just on my way out and saw your light on," she said, suddenly feeling uneasy.

"Tess is always the first one in and the last to leave,"

Owen told Jared. "And not just a dedicated worker but an incredibly talented one."

While Tess appreciated the words of praise, she couldn't help but wonder why her boss thought Jared McCabe would care about her work habits. But now wasn't the time for her to ask that question, so she only said, "I didn't mean to interrupt." Then, to Jared, "It was nice meeting you, Mr. McCabe."

He smiled again. "It was my pleasure, Ms. Lucas."

"Enjoy your weekend," Owen said.

Tess nodded, her mind swirling with questions about the mysterious Mr. McCabe. Then she thought about her upcoming dinner with Craig and remembered she had bigger issues to worry about.

Chapter Three

It was after seven-thirty by the time Tess pulled into the visitor parking lot of Craig's building but she stayed in her car a few more minutes, psyching herself for the next round with him. She hated the awkwardness between them—hated feeling edgy, irritable, confused. But she knew that wasn't likely to change until they'd come to an agreement about her pregnancy and his role in their baby's life.

She also knew that if she was to have any chance of talking Craig out of this crazy marriage idea, she would have to stay calm and focused. She could admit that marriage was an option, but she needed to convince him that there were compelling reasons to disregard that option.

Friendship and chemistry are both solid foundations for a relationship.

She shook her head trying to block out the echo of his words in her mind.

And if we got married, our baby would have a family.

A family was the one thing she'd always wanted and the greatest gift she knew she could give to her child. And Craig knew her well enough to know it was the most tempting thing he could offer.

But if she gave in to temptation, what would it cost? What would a marriage of convenience do to their friendship? How could she risk the solid relationship they had for the illusion of something more?

Tess pushed aside the questions along with her trepidation as she climbed out of the car. She'd asked him to be her friend—she needed to remember that he was the best friend she had and not do anything to screw that up.

She greeted the doorman by name as she made her through the lobby. Nigel responded with a smile and a wave, reaching for the phone to call Craig's apartment and let him know she was on her way up.

Craig opened the door just as she stepped off the elevator.

"Sorry, I'm later than I expected to be," she said. "I got caught up with Owen as I was on my way out." She considered mentioning the odd encounter with the stranger but decided that could wait until later.

"Not a problem," he said. "I'm a little behind schedule myself because of an impromptu visit from my mother."

"I'm sorry I missed her," Tess said, kicking off her shoes inside the entrance before following him into the kitchen.

"No, you're not."

She frowned.

"Long story," he said. "And right now I'm going to put the grill on so we can eat soon."

"Can I help you with anything?" she asked.

"You can throw the salad together if you want." He gestured to the ingredients on the counter.

"Okay." She washed the lettuce and began tearing it into pieces. She'd really hoped that having dinner with Craig tonight would be a step toward getting their relationship back on track, toward the resumption of their friendship. But she couldn't deny that being alone with him here—for the first time since the night their baby had been conceived—filled her with foreboding.

Truthfully, she was more afraid of her own reactions to him than anything he might say or do. Ever since the night they'd spent together, every little touch sent tingles of awareness through her veins. Even the briefest contact taunted her with the recollection of how it felt to *really* be touched by him.

She forced the memories aside and began slicing the cucumber with a vengeance. Craig came into the kitchen, picked up the plate of steaks. As he moved past her, she caught the scent of his aftershave. Once familiar and comforting, it was suddenly new and arousing. She brought the knife down hard, as if the action could sever her wayward thoughts—and cut her finger instead.

"Damn!" She stuck her finger in her mouth to staunch the flow of blood.

He set the plate back on the counter with a clatter. "Are you all right?"

He grabbed her wrist, his fingers strong and firm as he tugged her hand away from her mouth. With his other hand, he turned on the faucet and shoved her finger under the stream of cool water.

"I'm fine," she said, her voice strangely breathy. He was standing close, so close she could feel the heat emanating from his body. Too close.

He moved her hand out of the water to inspect the cut. It was still bleeding, but it wasn't very deep.

"Keep it under the water," he said. "I'll get a Band-Aid."

She did as he requested, too shaken to do anything else.

Craig was her best friend—she shouldn't be indulging in sexual daydreams with him cast in the starring role. But maybe the erotic images that haunted her were a result of the hormonal changes of pregnancy. Yes, that made sense. Once she had this baby, her relationship with Craig would settle back to normal. The next eight months might be a challenge, but she was confident she could get through them knowing that this fierce attraction was a temporary phenomenon.

Craig returned with a tube of antibacterial ointment and a Band-Aid, and she breathed in his scent again. He tore a paper towel off the roll and carefully dried her hand. Her finger, almost numb from the cold water, was infused with heat by the simple touch. Damn, it was going to be a long eight months.

"Okay?" he asked.

She nodded, then glanced up. And saw the awareness she felt reflected in the depths of his brown eyes. If this attraction was a temporary phenomenon, apparently it was affecting him, too.

But then he tore his gaze away from her to pick up the tube of cream and she managed to breathe again. His motions were brisk, efficient and so completely impersonal Tess wondered if she'd imagined the sizzle in the air between them.

He wrapped the Band-Aid around her finger. "There you go."

She swallowed. "Th-thank you."

"I'm going to put the steaks on." His smile seemed strained. "Try not to cut off any appendages while I'm gone."

Craig flipped the meat on the grill, listened to the sizzle and pop as the marinade dripped onto the hot coals. It reminded him of the heat that had flared between him and Tess when he'd touched her. He'd tried to keep the contact casual, impersonal, but the skin of her hand was soft in his and the scent of her hair tantalized his senses. And as he'd leaned over her by the sink administering first aid to her bleeding finger, he couldn't help but notice how the soft fabric of her blouse molded to the curve of her breasts. And he couldn't help but remember how those breasts had filled his palms, how she'd moaned in pleasure as he'd caressed them, with his hands, with his lips.

He breathed deeply of the cool night air as he willed the haunting images away. Tess would hardly be impressed if she knew about his prurient fantasies.

He was supposed to be her friend—and he had been, for fifteen years. There had been times in recent years that he'd wondered whether there could be anything more between them, but he'd always discarded the thought. He valued her friendship and he didn't want to do anything to risk it. No matter how many times he'd wondered what it would be like to touch her, to kiss her, and not like a friend.

Now he knew—and he knew that being friends wasn't enough anymore.

It was a huge leap from one night together to marriage, and he knew it wasn't a commitment he'd be considering now except for the fact of Tess's pregnancy. But instead of feeling trapped by the circumstances, he felt as if he'd been given an incredible opportunity. If only he could find a way to convince Tess of that fact.

He kept the conversation light and casual during dinner, and she finally seemed to relax a little. At least until he inadvertently brushed his knee against her thigh under the table. Then she jerked away as if he'd stabbed her with his steak knife, and he accepted that easing the tension between them wasn't going to be that simple.

"I've got Chunky Monkey for dessert," he said.

She loaded the dishwasher while he scooped her favorite ice cream into bowls. When he was finished, he decided that it was time to get to the purpose of her visit.

"You know that I wanted you to come over tonight so we could finish talking about my proposal."

Tess took the bowl he handed to her, passed him a spoon she'd taken out of the cutlery drawer. "I don't recall hearing an actual proposal."

Craig followed her to the table, enjoying the gentle sway of her hips as she moved. Then her response registered and he frowned. "What do you mean?"

She dipped her spoon into the ice cream. "You didn't ask me to marry you. You said we should get married."

He watched her lips close around the spoon, heard her soft hum of pleasure as she tasted the ice cream. He shoved a spoonful into his own mouth, hoping that the cold substance would help alleviate the heat raging through his system. It didn't work.

"I asked," he said.

"No, you didn't. You never ask," she continued. "You just assume you'll get what you want."

"I do not," he protested indignantly.

"Yes, you do. Because nobody ever says no to Craig Richmond."

As he scooped up some more ice cream, he realized she might be right. As Vice President in charge of Research and Development at Richmond Pharmaceuticals, he held a position of power and he knew how to wield that power effectively, but he'd never realized that his professional demeanor carried over to his private life.

Was that why she'd turned him down, because he hadn't asked?

He swallowed another mouthful of ice cream. "All right. Tess, will you marry me?"

She smiled but shook her head. "No."

"No?" So much for her theory that no one ever said no to him.

"I didn't refuse your so-called proposal because it wasn't in the form of a question," she told him. "I refused because my pregnancy isn't a good enough reason for us to get married."

Tess swirled her spoon in her ice cream, then licked the back of it. And he nearly groaned aloud at the erotic images the action evoked.

"I would never deny you access to our child," she said, drawing his attention back to the topic of conversation. "And I'm not going to marry a man I don't love and who doesn't love me just so my child will have a family when we can accomplish the same thing by sharing custody."

"I don't want to be a weekend dad." He couldn't stand the thought of his child being shuffled between households, never feeling as if he truly had a home, somewhere that he belonged. He didn't want his child to grow up thinking his father didn't want to be part of his life. He scrubbed a hand through his hair. "Why can't you accept that this is important to me?"

"Why can't you accept that I don't want to get married?"

"Because you were addressing wedding invitations not six months ago," he pointed out.

"That was different," she told him.

"Because you thought you were in love with Roger?"

"Maybe I was wrong about him, but that doesn't mean I'm willing to give up my dreams and settle for a loveless marriage."

He pushed his empty bowl aside. "Did you ever tell your fiancé that you spent four years of your life in foster care?"

She frowned. "What does that have to do with anything?"

"It doesn't change the fact that he was cheating scum and he didn't deserve you," he told her. "But I have to wonder if the relationship wasn't doomed anyway because you didn't let him see who you really are."

"Four years in foster care didn't make me who I am."

"A friend once told me that everything we experience in life—the good and the bad—helps to make us the people we are."

She shrugged, unable to argue against her own words. "Do you have a point?"

"Did he know about the foster homes?" he asked again. "Did he know how your mother died? How completely alone you felt when you realized her death made you an orphan? Did he know how much you looked forward to the monthly visits you were allowed with your stepsister, because she was the only family you had left?" He shook his head, then answered his own questions. "Of course he didn't know because you never told him."

"I didn't think it was relevant," she said.

"Or maybe you're more wary of commitment than I am. You say you're holding out for love, but maybe that's just an excuse to be alone because you're too afraid of being hurt again to let anyone get that close."

"I didn't know you got a psych degree along with your MBA."

The dripping sarcasm in her voice proved that he'd made his point. He only regretted that he'd hurt her in the process.

"I don't need a pysch degree because I know you," he reminded her gently.

She sighed. "Okay. Maybe you're right. Maybe I'm as much a coward as you are a commitment-phobe. Which suggests to me that a marriage between us would be doomed from the start."

"Except that we're also both stubborn and determined," he reminded her. "If we wanted to, we could make it work."

She set the spoon down, looked up at him and he saw the conviction in her deep blue eyes. "I remember what kind of marriage my parents had, how much they loved each other. I was only eight when my dad died but I remember how happy they were together.

"When my mother married Ken, I knew right away it was different. She was on her own with me, he was on his own with Laurie. They married to give us—me and Laurie—a family, but neither of them was ever really happy."

"That doesn't mean we couldn't be," he persisted.

"If I get married, I want it to be because someone wants to be with *me*, not because I'm carrying his child."

"I do want to be with you, Tess. I want us both to be there for our baby. I don't know how this love thing works. I'm not even sure I believe it exists—not love of the happily-ever-after variety, anyway. But I want this baby to know he has two parents who will always be there for him, and the best way to ensure that is by getting married."

She placed a hand over her chest. "I think that's the most romantic proposal I've heard yet."

He felt the frustration building inside him. "Is that what you want—romance?" he demanded. "Would it make a difference if I filled the room with flowers and soft music and candlelight?"

"No," she said again and shook her head. "Nothing is going to make a difference because we both know it would be worse for our child to live in a loveless home than to have two parents who never married."

"We could make a marriage work, Tess."

"Do you really want to take that chance? Do you want our child to find himself in the middle of a custody battle if it doesn't?"

"No, I don't," he admitted, understanding that she

was only thinking about what he and his brother had gone through. "But that wouldn't happen because we would always do what was best for our child."

"That's why I want to work out the details of custody and access now."

"I don't want access," he said stubbornly. "I want my child to know he's an important part of my life every day, not just on alternate weekends."

"Is this about Charlene walking out on you?"

She never referred to the woman who'd given birth to him as his mother, because she felt—as he did—that Grace, his father's second wife, was more of a mother to him than Charlene had ever been.

"This is about you and me and our baby," he insisted.

But Tess—being Tess—didn't accept his denial. She reached across the table and laid her hand on top of his.

"Charlene couldn't handle the responsibility of having children," she said. "But you've made it clear that you want to be a part of our baby's life, and I would never stand in the way of that."

He turned his hand over, laced his fingers with hers. Her hand was so small inside his and yet he drew comfort and strength from her presence, gained a measure of peace from her understanding. She knew him better than anyone, she understood his hopes and fears and she was always there for him. It was the kind of unconditional acceptance he'd never been sure of with any other woman, and yet another reason he believed they would make a marriage work.

But she was holding out for love, and as much as he cared about her, that wasn't something he could give her. If he could love anyone, he wanted to believe it would be Tess. But he didn't have it in him. And he wouldn't lie to her—he wouldn't use the words she wanted to hear to get what he wanted. Or maybe he just knew better than to even try because Tess would see right through him.

She gave his hand a reassuring squeeze. "You're going to be a wonderful daddy, Craig."

"Don't you mean part-time daddy?" He hated to think about missing a single day of his child's life. He'd been five years old when his parents split up, but he remembered the feeling of loss, the sense of rejection when his mother walked out on them.

It had been months later before Charlene Richmond had decided she wanted to share custody of her children—or maybe she finally realized that by having them live with her part-time, she could get significant financial support from her husband. And the next few years had been a constant shuffle from one house to the other for Craig and his brother, Gage, the only consistent presence in their life being the nanny their father had hired and who accompanied them from place to place. Because as much as Charlene claimed she wanted to spend time with her sons, she was content to let the nanny deal with their day-to-day needs and, in fact, rarely interacted with them during their visits.

Then, one day when they showed up, she just wasn't there. All she'd left was a note saying that she was getting married and moving out of the country and was, therefore, relinquishing full custody to the boys' father.

At first, Craig had been relieved—the fighting would finally stop and he and Gage would finally be able to settle in one place. But the relief had soon been replaced by a niggling fear that his father might decide to go away, too. That no one loved him enough to stand by him.

He wouldn't let his child feel the same way.

As much as Tess understood Craig's reasons for wanting to get married, she wasn't willing to sacrifice what was left of their friendship and give up her own dreams for a marriage of convenience she believed was destined to fail.

But when he looked at her as he was looking at her now, with such intensity and determination, she could feel her resolve weakening. Then he stroked his thumb over her skin and she felt a frisson of awareness skate up her arm and warmth spread through her body.

She tried to pull her hand away, knowing that if she had any hopes of maintaining a clear perspective on things, she couldn't allow him to touch her. But Craig held firm.

"I've tried not to pressure you—"

She almost laughed at the absurdity of the statement as she felt the pressure closing in on her from all sides.

"—but you can't keep your pregnancy a secret forever. Let's go away somewhere and get married before the speculation begins."

And despite all her reasoning and common sense she actually found herself tempted by the idea. Because the thought of having this baby on her own, of being—if not solely, at least primarily—responsible for its happiness and well-being, terrified her. But she'd never been the type to balk at a challenge or take the easy way out and she wasn't going to do so now just because she was scared.

She carefully withdrew her hand from his grasp. "I can't marry you, Craig."

"Think about this logically," he said. "We've known each other for years. What we have between us—friendship, trust, respect—they're more important than love. And more enduring. There's no reason for a marriage between us not to work."

She didn't buy his argument. Yes, friendship, trust and respect were important, but she wouldn't enter into a marriage without love. "Look at your parents. Your dad and Grace," she amended. "It's obvious to anyone who sees them together that they love one another. Do you really want to settle for less than that?"

"I would never think of marrying you as settling," he said.

He sounded so sincere and was looking at her with such earnestness in his dark eyes that Tess almost believed him. In her heart, she wanted to believe him. But her disastrous experience with Roger had made her wary. And while she'd known Craig a lot longer than she'd known Roger, so much had changed between them in the last few weeks that she wasn't sure she really knew him at all anymore.

At work she was a confident, competent professional but that was because she'd spent years studying manuals and mastering computer code. There was no such training to succeed at relationships and she felt at a distinct disadvantage when it came to the games that men and women played.

Craig, on the other hand, had dated more women than she could count—beautiful, sophisticated women. He would never be happy with someone like her and she'd be deluding herself if she believed otherwise for a single moment.

Tess sighed and pushed away from the table. She crossed over to the window, looked out at the brilliant array of stars scattered across the sky. No, there was no way she could marry Craig.

"You might not think of it that way now," she said. "But you'd eventually start to resent me, and the baby, for putting you in this position."

And for Tess, the thought of losing Craig's friendship and support was far worse than the prospect of raising a child on her own.

He didn't say anything for a minute and she let herself hope he was actually considering what she'd said. She didn't hear him leave the table, wasn't aware that he was behind her until he put his hands on her shoulders and gently turned her around to face him.

She met his gaze evenly, almost defiantly. She knew him well enough to know that he wasn't easily dissuaded from something he wanted, but she could be equally stubborn. And there was no way she was going to further jeopardize their friendship by marrying him. Her mom and Ken had been friends before they married and they'd had nothing left when their marriage had fallen apart. Tess refused to let that happen. Craig could use whatever arguments he wanted, she wasn't going to change her mind.

But his response wasn't at all what she expected. He didn't argue or plead or use any of the other tactics she was confident she could handle. Instead, he lowered his head and he kissed her.

At first, she was too stunned to react. And then, as

his lips continued to move over hers, soft but firm, strong yet coaxing, she simply melted.

He slid his fingers into her hair and tipped her head back to deepen the kiss. She opened for him willingly, all thoughts of resistance gone. Whether it was the pregnancy hormones running rampant through her system or her new awareness of Craig as a man, she had no desire to be anywhere but in his arms.

She shivered as his fingers massaged her scalp, moaned as his tongue tangled with hers. Somewhere, in the back recesses of her mind, she knew she should end this kiss. She shouldn't allow this to happen but she was powerless to stop the desire that flowed hot and thick through her system. She wanted this—she wanted Craig—more than she'd ever thought possible.

He stroked his hands down her back, tugged the blouse from the waistband of her slacks, and she trembled with anticipation. Then his hands were on her skin and she could no longer think. She could only feel and she loved the way it felt to be touched by him, to touch him. She ran her hands up his chest, found the buttons at the front of his shirt and quickly worked them free.

He slid an arm behind her knees and scooped her up, cradling her against his chest as his lips continued their sensual assault. She'd never been swept off her feet before—literally or figuratively—and if she let herself think about it she might worry that Craig was her first on both counts and that it felt so completely right.

He carried her into the living room, laid her down gently on the soft leather sofa and levered himself down beside her. Their bodies were aligned, their legs entwined, on the narrow couch. She could feel the evidence of his arousal against her belly and wriggled her hips to position him between her thighs.

Her blouse was undone now, too, and he slid the garment over her shoulders, letting it drop to the ground. Then he shifted their bodies so that she was lying beneath him and dipped his head to nuzzle her throat, the scrape of his jaw against her tender skin sending deliciously erotic tingles through her body.

His lips moved lower, caressing the swell of her breasts above the lacy cups of her bra. She felt her nipples tighten, the heat spread through her body. As if in response to an unspoken request, he flicked his tongue over the aching peak, then closed his teeth over the thin fabric. Tess gasped and thrust her hips upward. Impatiently Craig pushed the strap off her shoulder and took her nipple in his mouth. He manipulated the peak, tasting, teasing, then he suckled hard on the breast, thrusting it against the roof of his mouth with his tongue. She bit down on her lip to keep from crying out as she rocked her hips against him, aching for the fulfillment of his lovemaking.

"Let me make love with you, Tess."

His words paralleled her thoughts, proving they were—if at odds over everything else—at least in synch in their desire for one another.

She gripped his shoulders with trembling hands. "Yes."

He undid the button of her slacks, slid the zipper down. His fingers found the wet heat inside her and she almost flew apart right then.

"Let me remind you how good we are together," he whispered the words against her lips as his hands continued to tease and torment her. "Let me show you how wonderful it would be to make love every night if we got married."

It took a minute for his words to penetrate through the fog that surrounded Tess's brain. When they did, the heat flowing through her veins suddenly chilled.

"What..." She had to pause for breath, forced herself to ignore the traitorous demands of her body that insisted his words didn't matter. "What did you say?"

He leaned forward again and brushed his lips against hers, softly coaxing. "I said I want to make love with you."

She wanted to melt against him, to lean into the kiss, to go back to where she'd been before she'd heard the words that had doused her own desire more effectively than an icy rain. "Why?"

He smiled, that slow, sexy smile that made her insides all trembly and weak. "I thought that was obvious."

"Is it?" She felt her cheeks flush but wouldn't allow herself to be distracted by his easy charm. Not again.

Instead, she pushed herself up and scrambled off of the couch. She found her discarded top and shoved her arms through the sleeves, turning her back on him to fasten the buttons and zip up her slacks. It wasn't about modesty so much as hiding the hurt she was afraid he'd see in her eyes when she spoke her next words. "Or was this part of your plan to convince me to marry you?"

She heard him sigh. "I didn't plan this at all, Tess, things just got out of control. But to be perfectly honest, I think the attraction between us is further proof that our marriage would succeed."

She turned back to him, confident that any residual hurt would be shrouded by the anger that was beginning to boil inside her. "We should get married because we're good in bed together?"

He stood up and took a step toward her. "We're a lot better than good, but that's only one factor."

"That's what this was to you?" She impatiently brushed away the tears that spilled onto her cheeks. "A factor?"

"Of course not," he denied.

But she knew him well enough to recognize the guilt that flickered in his eyes. Tess straightened her shirt.

"Go to hell, and take your proposal with you."

Chapter Four

Tess wasn't really surprised that she didn't hear from Craig through the following week, but she was sorry. He'd been the one person she'd always felt she could count on and she'd screwed it up by, well, screwing him. It was crude but true. Have sex with a guy once and it changed *everything*. And now, when she needed his support more than ever, he was conspicuously absent from her life.

More than a month had passed since she'd taken the home pregnancy test and though she'd scheduled her first prenatal appointment, she still didn't know what was the best thing to do for her baby. What she did know was that she'd drive herself insane if she continued to stare at the same four walls inside her apartment. So Saturday morning, with no destination in mind, she climbed in her Saturn coupe and drove. When she found herself in the west end of town, she decided to drop in on her sister.

Technically, Laurie was Tess's stepsister but neither of them had any biological siblings and the relationship they'd developed over the years was as strong as any made by blood. Although the marriage between their respective parents hadn't worked out, the girls had stayed in touch after the divorce. Laurie was the only other person Tess could imagine confiding in about her current situation, and right now she desperately needed to confide in someone.

"It's not even 10:00 a.m.," Laurie complained as she pulled open the front door.

Tess held up the tray of coffee and the box of doughnuts. "I brought breakfast."

Laurie stepped away from the door and Tess followed her into the kitchen. She set the doughnuts and coffee on the table, then scooped ten-week-old Devin out of his infant carrier. She always loved spending time with her sister's kids, had always dreamed of having a baby of her own someday. Now that day was on the horizon.

"I can't believe how much he's grown." Her voice was filled with awe as she stared at the chubby infant cradled in her arms.

Laurie smiled. "He's gained five pounds already."

"Is that normal?" she asked, struck once again by how little she knew about babies, how much she needed to learn.

"The doctor likes to see newborns gain at least a pound a month, so he's a little ahead of schedule."

She brushed a kiss on the soft, downy head, breathed in his soft, baby scent. "Already an over-achiever, aren't you?"

The baby, of course, didn't respond.

But then his big sister wandered into the kitchen.

"Juice, mommy." Two-year-old Becca waved a plastic cup at her mother.

"Please," Laurie told her, taking the cup.

Becca shook her head no. "Ap-ple."

Tess smiled as the child's mother shook her head.

"She doesn't quite understand 'please' and 'thank you' yet," Laurie explained as she took the juice from the refrigerator and refilled the cup. Becca took the cup back to the living room where she'd been playing with the building blocks scattered across the carpet.

"What does Becca think of her little brother?" Tess asked.

"It varies from day to day, although usually she just ignores him. Once he's big enough to actually play with, I suspect that will change." Laurie sat down on the other side of the table and took one of the paper cups from the tray. She removed the lid and smiled as she inhaled deeply. "Cappuccino. I guess I'll have to forgive you for arriving before noon."

"I am sorry for dropping by without calling first," she apologized. "But I really need to talk to you about something."

Her sister waved off the apology. "You know you're always welcome—and I'm always starved for adult conversation."

Tess managed a smile as she stroked a hand lightly over Devin's soft, downy head. He'd already settled against her breast and was sleeping soundly. In less than eight months, she'd be able to cradle her own baby this way. The realization filled her with a strange sort of longing and almost none of the panic she'd learned to expect since her pregnancy was confirmed. "Where's Dave?"

"Grocery shopping." Laurie passed the other cup of coffee to her. "He won't be back for at least half an hour. Now stop procrastinating and tell me what's up."

"I'm pregnant."

Her sister choked on a mouthful of coffee, sputtered. "Pregnant?"

Tess nodded.

Laurie considered the revelation for a long moment before she said, "I didn't realize you'd been dating anyone…since Roger."

"I wasn't. I'm not." She felt her cheeks burn. "It's Craig's baby."

"Craig Richmond?"

"Yeah."

Laurie took a cautious sip of her cappuccino. "Well, this is an interesting development."

"Interesting is one word for it," Tess agreed dryly. *"Insanity* is another."

"And I thought you were insane for not going after him years ago," her sister teased.

Tess frowned; Laurie grinned.

"So what was the cause of this insanity?" she asked, reaching into the box for a chocolate doughnut.

"The wedding that didn't happen." Tess bit into her jelly-filled and chewed as she considered how to explain something she wasn't entirely sure she understood herself. "I thought Roger was the one," she said softly. "I thought I'd finally met the man with whom I'd spend the rest of my life. That we'd get married and have children and—well, you know that story."

"Actually, I never understood what you saw in that guy," Laurie said.

"I thought you liked him."

Her sister shrugged. "I wanted *you* to be happy."

She sighed. "Instead, on the night that should have been my wedding night, I ended up at a bar having a few drinks." She looked away, embarrassed by the recklessness of her behavior. "And then a good-looking guy sat beside me at the bar and asked me to dance and I was feeling lonely enough to accept his invitation."

"And?"

"And we danced." She took another bite of her doughnut. "And he was starting to hint that he wanted to do a whole lot more when Craig came into the bar. He told me later that he saw my car in the parking lot and was worried about me. My fault, I guess, for picking a bar on his side of town." And she wondered now whether that had been mere coincidence or a subconscious choice. "Anyway, he took me home."

"I can't believe Craig would take advantage of you in that situation," she said indignantly.

"He wouldn't. He didn't. He only wanted to take me home." Devin stirred in his sleep, and Tess gently rubbed his back until he settled again. "But I didn't want to go home. I didn't want to be alone."

"So he took you back to his place," Laurie guessed.

"He held me while I cried." She picked up her coffee again. "And then he kissed me."

Laurie waited, obviously expecting more of an explanation, but Tess had no intention of traveling any farther down memory lane. Not when the events of that night still haunted her dreams.

"Kissing doesn't make babies," Laurie said at last.

Tess managed a smile. "No, but since you've had two of your own, I didn't figure you needed a complete play-by-play."

"Not all the details—but I get the feeling you're holding something back."

She sighed a little wistfully. "Just that it was the single most incredible experience of my life. Never in a million years would I have imagined that sex could be so…so…everything."

"It is when it's with the right person," her sister agreed.

"He's not the right person," Tess denied. "Not for me."

"Why not?"

"Because we're friends."

"Obviously a little more than friends," Laurie commented.

Tess ignored the sarcasm and concentrated on finishing her doughnut.

"What did Craig say about the baby?"

She wiped the powdered sugar off her fingers with a paper napkin. "He offered to marry me."

Her sister smiled. "When's the wedding?"

Tess scowled. "What makes you think I'd say yes?"

"Because you'd have to be crazy not to. He's a wonderful man—gorgeous and sexy, smart and rich. You've had phenomenal sex together and he's your best friend. Most marriages don't start out with so much going for them."

"But he only offered to marry me because I'm pregnant."

"Which shows that he's also responsible and honorable."

"I *can't* marry him," Tess insisted.

"Why not?"

"Because I recently escaped one near-matrimonial disaster and am not particularly anxious to rush into another."

"What makes you think that marriage to Craig would be a disaster?"

"Because he doesn't deserve to be trapped into a marriage he doesn't really want and because I don't need a husband to have this baby."

Devin stirred again and brought his fist to his mouth to suck on it.

"Maybe you don't need a husband," Laurie admitted after a long pause. "But having grown up without a father yourself, don't you want one for your child?"

She sighed; her sister always knew what buttons to push. "Of course I *want* my baby to have a father. But wanting and having aren't always the same thing. And I don't ever want Craig to resent this baby or to hate me because he was trapped into marriage."

"Honey, Craig is not the type of man to be trapped into anything. If he didn't want to marry you, he wouldn't have offered."

"I'm not sure he wants to marry me," Tess said. "He wants to be a father."

"He doesn't have to marry you to be a father to his child."

Which was exactly the point Tess had tried to make to him.

"Maybe his reasons for wanting to marry you go deeper than you know," Laurie suggested.

Tess shook her head. "No, he was very clear on why he wants to get married."

"Oh." Her sister was obviously disappointed. "What are you going to do?"

"I'm going to have this baby, on my own and I'm going to hope that Craig and I can salvage our friendship."

"Are you sure that's what you want?"

Tess wasn't sure about anything anymore—except that it was nearly impossible to think about Craig as a friend when she could still remember how it felt to have her naked body joined with his, when she yearned to experience that sense of closeness and completion again. But no matter how compelling the physical attraction was, she knew marriage wasn't the answer. Although it might solve some of her immediate problems, it wasn't a viable long-term solution.

"At this point, I think it's the best I can hope for," she said.

"Do you want to know what I think?" Laurie asked.

"Probably not," she admitted, "but you might as well tell me anyway."

"I think you're afraid you could fall in love with him."

"If I was going to fall in love with Craig, it wouldn't have taken fifteen years to happen," she pointed out.

"There's no statute of limitations on love."

She shook her head.

"Now that I think about it," her sister continued, "it makes perfect sense. You've always dated men who let you set the boundaries of the relationship and you never let any of them get close enough to touch your heart. I used to worry that you were afraid to fall in love—because of the mess your mom and my dad made of their marriage. But now I wonder if you maintained that emotional distance because you were already in love with Craig."

"I loved Roger," Tess said.

"You *wanted* to be in love with Roger," Laurie said. "Because you didn't want to admit your feelings for Craig."

"I'm *not* in love with Craig."

"You're not the type of person to act on impulse," her sister pointed out. "But somehow you ended up in bed with Craig and I don't think that ever would have happened unless you harbored some pretty strong feelings for the guy. And if that's true, marrying him wouldn't be such a bad thing."

"I thought you'd be on my side," Tess said peevishly.

"I am on your side," her sister promised her. "I just want you to be happy."

She remained silent, willing her to let the subject drop.

But Laurie wasn't going to do so without one last remark. "I think you could be happy with Craig—if you give yourself a chance."

Tess was grateful when her niece's chants of "Da-dee" interrupted their conversation.

"Da-dee, Da-dee." Becca repeated, racing toward the door as a key turned in the lock.

Tess watched as her brother-in-law, in a smooth and obviously well-practiced move, shifted the grocery bags he carried to one hand and scooped the child up in his free arm as he stepped through the door.

Dave kissed his daughter's cheek loudly. "How's my girl?"

At the sound of his father's voice, Devin's eyes

opened wide and he tried to twist his head around. Tess turned the baby in her arms so that he could see the father he obviously adored as much as his sister did.

She remembered the excitement she'd always felt when her father came home at the end of the day: the comforting feel of his strong hugs, the familiar scent of his spicy cologne. Along with the warmth of the memory came a pang of guilt. Did she have the right to deprive her baby of the same thing?

She forced the question—and the doubts—from her mind as Dave set Becca back on her feet and carried the groceries into the kitchen. The kiss he gave his wife was long and lingering. Tess looked away, her heart sighing. It was obvious that Laurie and Dave were very much in love and very happy together, and Tess was genuinely happy for them—if just a little bit envious.

This was what she wanted: a husband who loved her, a family they could raise together. But the fairy tale was out of her reach. Reality was an unplanned pregnancy and a proposed marriage of convenience from her best friend.

After Tess had stormed out of his apartment the previous Friday night, Craig knew she'd need some time and distance to cool off. Because he'd recognized that she was truly ticked—Tess using any kind of swear word was a clear indication of that—he'd given her a full week. But he didn't want to let it go much longer than that without making things right between them again.

He wanted to get back to the place where he could call her at any time of the day just to say hi or stop by her apartment on a whim just because he wanted to see her. He hadn't truly understood how much he looked forward to talking to her and seeing her until he'd forced himself to take a step back and found that she was his first thought every morning and the last before he went to bed at night.

He'd spent the better part of the week considering how to approach her and had at last come up with a plan. Unfortunately, when he finally went over to her apartment Saturday morning to implement it, Tess wasn't home.

But Craig wasn't going to give up that easily.

It was almost noon when she returned and found him waiting in her living room.

"How did you get in here?" she demanded.

"I used the key you gave me."

Her gaze narrowed. "The key I gave to you in case of an *emergency*?"

"I thought it was an emergency," he told her. "I tried calling all morning and you never answered."

"Obviously I wasn't here."

"Well, I didn't know that until I came over," he pointed out. "Because usually you have your cell phone when you're out and you weren't answering that, either."

"I forgot to turn it on when I went out," she admitted.

"A few things on your mind?"

She ignored the jibe. "So you came over here and let yourself in—"

"I knocked first," he felt compelled to interrupt in his own defense. He could tell that she was annoyed with him and getting more annoyed by the minute, and he was worried he wouldn't get a chance to apologize before she kicked him out.

"Okay," she conceded. "You knocked and then you let yourself in. But why—when you realized I wasn't here and there wasn't any kind of emergency—didn't you leave?"

"Because I'd already ordered the flowers and thought someone should be here to accept delivery."

She looked around, as if only now noticing the bouquets of roses that he'd set around the room. There were vases of red and pink and white and yellow and peach and lavender and something the florist called bicolor roses. He'd ordered a dozen of every color, hoping the extravagant display would soften Tess's heart toward him.

"I told you I didn't want flowers," she said. "And filling my apartment with them isn't going to change my mind."

But she didn't sound quite so annoyed anymore, and she picked up the vase of white roses to sniff the fragrant blooms.

"These aren't a lead-in to another marriage proposal, they're an apology."

Her lips curved slightly as she glanced around at the colorful display. "You must be very sorry."

"Sorrier than you can know."

She touched the petal of one of the purple flowers. "I have to admit, I like this kind of apology. But I'd also like to know what you're apologizing for."

"I'm not sorry I kissed you," he admitted. "I'm not sorry we almost made love—well, actually I *am* sorry it was only an almost. But I'm mostly sorry that you thought I was trying to manipulate you."

"Weren't you?"

He couldn't help but smile. "Sometimes you give me too much credit, Tess. The truth is, what happened wasn't a planned seduction but simple runaway lust."

"Really?"

She seemed relieved to know that he couldn't contain his desire for her, which was ironic because the same realization completely unnerved him.

"Really," he assured her. And he'd figured that if he couldn't be alone with Tess without wanting his hands on her, he'd just make sure they weren't alone together. Or he'd keep a ten-foot distance between them at all times.

"Then I guess I do forgive you."

"Thank you."

She smiled. "Thank you for the flowers, even if they were an unnecessarily extravagant gesture."

He exhaled a silent sigh, certain they'd taken the first step toward reestablishing the camaraderie that had meant so much to him over the years and hoping that his next words wouldn't undo the progress they'd made.

"I still think we should get married, but obviously we don't agree on that, so I'd like us to at least work together to do what's best for the baby."

"I'd like that, too," she said.

"And I thought that going to a movie tonight would be a step in the right direction. There's a new James Bond film playing downtown."

Tess hesitated, although she wasn't sure why. She was a huge James Bond fan and she and Craig had gone to the movies together plenty of times before. But there was something about his deliberate casualness and apparent acquiescence that sent up warning flags in her mind.

"Do you already have plans?" he asked when she didn't immediately respond.

"No," she admitted.

"It's just a movie," he said in a matter-of-fact tone she knew was meant to be reassuring.

But she knew Craig too well to trust that his motives were as simple as he claimed. "Just a movie?"

"And maybe a bite to eat after," he added.

She hesitated another moment before giving in— because she really did want to see the movie. "Okay."

He smiled. "Great. I've got some errands to run this afternoon, but I'll come back to pick you up around seven."

"Or I could meet you at the theater," she suggested.

"I'll pick you up," he said again. "It's more appropriate for a first date."

"It's not a date," she said.

His smile only widened. "I know it's a little unorthodox, considering that you're already pregnant with my baby, but I thought we should have a few dates before we discuss marriage."

And which confirmed what she'd feared—Craig had not given up.

"I thought you agreed that marriage was out—that we were going to work together to do what's best for the baby."

"No," he denied. "I only agreed that we *dis*agreed about marriage and this is what's best for our baby."

"Maybe this isn't such a good idea."

"I'll see you at seven," he said, already on his way to the door.

"I think we need to talk about this some more."

"We can talk tonight."

"Wait, Craig—"

Her entreaty was cut off by the click of the door closing behind him.

Tess huffed out an exasperated breath, wondering what exactly she'd agreed to.

Chapter Five

A ten-foot distance, Craig decided later, wasn't a realistic option when a man was trying to court a woman. And the simple act of sharing popcorn with Tess was wreaking havoc on his self-control.

In the darkness of the theater, their attention occupied by the action on the screen, he reached into the bag and his knuckles brushed hers. He felt her hand pull away from the casual contact, sensed the stiffening in her shoulders. He withdrew his hand, munched on the popcorn. Her scent continued to tease his nostrils. So simple, so Tess and so utterly seductive.

He shifted uncomfortably in his seat and tried to focus on the movie. But all he could think about was the woman beside him. How she'd responded to his touch; how she'd opened up to him—not just her body, but her heart; and the feeling that he'd found a part of heaven when he'd buried himself inside her.

No, there was no way they could ever go back to being just friends again. It wasn't enough anymore.

But how was he ever going to convince Tess?

And why was it so critical that he do so?

He'd thought long and hard about the situation— he'd barely been able to think of anything else since he learned that she was going to have his baby. And he'd given serious consideration to her suggestion of shared custody. But in the end, he couldn't accept it. It wasn't what he wanted for their child and it wasn't what he wanted for him and Tess.

He wanted to be with her, to raise their child with her. He believed they could do it—build a life together, be happy together. He knew that she deserved more than a marriage based on friendship and parental responsibilities, but the reality was that she guarded her emotions as closely as he did.

They were both private people who didn't open up easily to others. And yet, they'd become the best of friends, sharing hopes and fears with one another that they'd never share with anyone else. He had no secrets from Tess. She knew him better than anyone—and she loved him anyway. As he loved her.

Okay, so maybe it wasn't the romantic kind of love Tess was looking for. But it was a comforting and comfortable feeling—because he knew that she was the one person who would always stand by him. And he would do the same for her.

The rustles and murmurs of people beginning to shuffle out of the theater distracted him from his thoughts. He looked up and frowned as he noticed the credits scrolling upward on the screen. He hadn't even realized the movie had ended, although he didn't doubt that James Bond had blown away the bad guys and got the girl. He always did.

Tess enjoyed the movie and she enjoyed being with Craig in the casual, relaxed atmosphere of the theater. She'd missed this—the comfortable friendship they'd shared for so many years—so much that she almost wished there was a way to go back to the time when they'd been just friends. But she wouldn't wish her baby away and she knew that things had started to change between them long before she woke up in his bed, anyway.

She pushed those thoughts and questions out of her mind and concentrated on the screen, but she jolted when his thigh pressed against hers, felt her pulse race in response to the casual brush of his fingertips if they met hers inside the bag of popcorn. By the time the picture of the embracing couple faded to black, Tess felt hot and tingly all over.

She'd seen dozens of movies with Craig over the years, maybe hundreds, and never before had her body been so attuned to every move of his. She was acting like a high school girl on a first date and she mentally damned him for putting that idea in her head. Except that she'd been fairly innocent in high school and had never imagined taking advantage of the darkened theater to straddle her date and have her way with him. She might be appalled that she was entertaining such thoughts now but she couldn't deny them.

But this is Craig, her conscience scolded. *Your best friend, the father of your baby.*

Okay, maybe she should try to forget the father of her baby part because her body was all too aware of how *that* had happened—and more than willing to do it again. Or maybe her body was responding so acutely to his because of the pregnancy. Yes, that made sense. She remembered reading somewhere that it wasn't unusual to experience an increase in sexual desire during pregnancy.

Obviously that's what she was feeling—it really had nothing to do with Craig specifically and everything to do with the hormonal changes in her body. Everything would go back to normal after the baby was born. All she had to do was stay out of Craig's bed—and keep him out of hers—in the interim.

Which was why she accepted his invitation to go for pizza after the movie was over—because she needed some time to cool off before he took her home and she dragged him inside with her and locked the door.

"Why is it that women can't resist James Bond?" Craig asked her as they were sharing a large pepperoni and three-cheese pizza at Marco's.

Tess smiled. "Because he's handsome, adventurous and daring."

"He's also reckless, ruthless and unfaithful."

"True," she admitted. "But he always saves the world."

"If I saved the world, would you marry me?"

She should have known better than to let her guard down, that Craig would eventually find a way to circle back to his own agenda. "James Bond never wants to marry the girl," she pointed out to him.

"You're avoiding my question."

"If the world needed to be saved, I'd rather do it my-self than rely on someone else to do it for me."

"What if you couldn't do it yourself?" he asked, se-lecting another slice of pizza.

"Are we still talking about saving the world or raising a baby?"

"I don't doubt you're capable of raising this baby on your own," he said. "I just wish you'd consider how much easier it would be for both of us if we shared the day-to-day responsibilities."

"I have considered it," she told him.

He looked up, obviously surprised by the admission.

"And I'll admit there are reasons I might consider marriage in these circumstances."

"Such as?" he prompted.

She unzipped her purse and pulled out a folded sheet of paper.

He stared at her. "You made a list?"

"I figured you'd want reasons and I wanted to make sure I'd considered all the pros and cons."

He took the page from her hand, unfolded it. "There are a lot more pros than cons," he noted with approval.

"Not every factor carries the same weight."

"Hmm." He scanned her notes, his lips curving. "You think I'm smart, fun and great in bed."

She snatched back the list and pointed to what she'd written in the other column. "I also noted that you have one enormous, intractable flaw."

"Not just good but great, huh?" His smile widened.

She huffed out an impatient breath. "Yes, okay, the sex was phenomenal. Now that we've stoked your ego, can we focus on what's relevant?"

"I think sexual attraction and physical compatibility are very relevant."

"So you've said before," she told him. "And so is your inability to commit to an adult relationship."

"Just because I've chosen not to make a commitment doesn't mean I'm not capable of commitment."

She nodded. "You're right. I almost forgot that you were engaged once. And that lasted what—all of three months?"

"You were engaged once, too," he reminded her.

"Yes, but I didn't just change my mind."

"I didn't change mine, either," he said. "I just realized that I'd let Lana steamroll me into an engagement I didn't want and I wasn't going to let her steamroll me into a marriage."

"Because you couldn't make a commitment."

"Because I didn't want to make a commitment to her."

"Your relationship with Lana ended two years ago and you haven't had a relationship that's lasted longer than a few weeks since then."

"That's not true," he said. "I dated Michelle Gable for almost four months."

Tess snorted. "She was the travel writer, wasn't she?"

"So?"

"So she was out of the country for at least half of that time."

"Okay," he relented. "Maybe I haven't wanted to make a commitment to anyone before. But I want to, now. I want to be with you, Tess, to be there for our children."

"*Child*," she corrected automatically. "Singular."

He looked at her with wide-eyed innocence. "Didn't I ever tell you that twins run in my family? On both sides."

"That's not funny."

"It's true." He held up his hand as if swearing an oath. "My maternal grandfather had a twin brother and my cousins, Kevin and Kayla, on my father's side are twins."

She wasn't sure she believed him. And even if he was telling the truth that didn't mean she would have twins.

But the mere possibility threw her. What if she was pregnant with twins? Two babies would mean twice as many feedings, twice as many dirty diapers, twice as much laundry. How would she handle all of that on her own?

She drew in a deep breath as she battled against the rising panic. She wasn't going to worry about something over which she had no control. Not yet, anyway. And not when she suspected that Craig was trying to make her panic—and run to him for help.

She gestured to the last slice on the tray and casually asked, "Do you want to finish that?"

"You go ahead," he said. "You might actually be eating for three these days."

Tess ignored him and bit into the pizza.

Grace Richmond inhaled the pungent aromas of garlic and oregano, her mouth already watering in anticipation of the spicy Italian sausage pizza she and Allan always shared when they came to Marco's. Saturday night was their usual date night. No matter how busy things were at the office for Allan or how involved Grace might be in whatever charitable committee she was currently assisting, they looked forward to spending this one evening together.

Today they'd gone to a pottery show at the local art gallery, then wandered through some of the downtown shops before taking in a movie at the Odyssey Theater. Allan had made reservations at their favorite French restaurant, but after the movie Grace hadn't been in the mood for a fancy meal and had suggested they stop by Marco's for a quick bite.

Allan had shaken his head in mock dismay that she would turn down five-star cuisine for pizza, but had graciously given in to her request. In all the years they'd been together, he'd given her everything she'd ever wanted and so much more than she'd ever dreamed of and her greatest wish was that both of their sons would find special women who could do the same for them.

Right now Gage wasn't anywhere near ready to settle down and though Craig hadn't shown any inclination to get serious with anyone since his broken engagement with Lana, she sensed that he needed the stability of a relationship. She worried that if he didn't find balance in his life soon, he would become too career-focused and settled in his ways to ever find a woman willing to put up with him.

As she glanced around the restaurant searching for a vacant table with thoughts of her eldest stepson on her mind, she saw him. At first she assumed it was just someone who looked like him, that she'd conjured his image because she'd been thinking of him. But then she recognized Tess sitting across from him.

She didn't think anything of it at first—after all, Craig and Tess had been friends for a long time—and she was actually going to suggest to Allan that they join the younger couple. Then she saw Craig reach across the table and touch Tess's hand, and Tess looked up at him and the sizzle in the air was almost tangible.

Grace took a mental step back, then a physical step. She didn't know what, if anything, was going on between Craig and Tess, but she didn't want to interfere, even inadvertently.

She squeezed Allan's hand as the hostess finally started toward them. "Let's go somewhere else to eat."

He turned and frowned at her. "I thought you wanted pizza."

"I changed my mind," she said.

He looked at her strangely.

She couldn't blame him and she couldn't explain why they needed to leave, she only knew that they did.

"I'd just rather go somewhere else. Or maybe we could pick something up on the way home." She leaned closer and dropped her voice so that no one would overhear. "Maybe something that can be heated up later."

She loved that he immediately understood what she was offering. She loved even more that after so many years together, his eyes still darkened at the thought of making love with her.

"Suddenly I'm not in the mood for pizza, either," he said, and led her back outside.

Tess was fixing glitches in a new software program Tuesday morning and wishing she could so easily fix the glitches in her life.

You could be happy with Craig.

Her sister's words echoed in her mind as they'd been

doing for the past three days and they tugged at her because she suspected that they were true.

She could be happy with Craig. As he'd pointed out when he first proposed the idea of marriage, they'd been friends for a long time and they shared common interests. But would that be enough to sustain a long-term relationship? Could she give up on her dream of falling in love and being loved in return? Could she fall in love with Craig? Or was she, as Laurie suspected, already in love with him?

She punched at the keyboard, reconfiguring the program, her fingers moving automatically as her mind continued on its wayward path.

She knew that Craig would be a wonderful father and that their child would benefit from having him around full-time. He'd probably be a great husband, too. Craig excelled at everything he did.

And he was offering her everything that she'd ever wanted: not just a baby, but a father for her child and a husband—a family. He would probably even complete the picture by finding a house with a white picket fence and a puppy to romp in the backyard. Yes, she could definitely be happy with that. It was the kind of life she'd been dreaming about since she was a little girl.

The tougher question was: could Craig be happy?

And it was her inability to answer that question with any degree of certainty that continued to hold her back.

When the phone rang on her desk, she reached eagerly for the receiver, grateful for the interruption of these disquieting thoughts.

"Hey, Tess."

She felt her pulse leap in recognition as Craig spoke. It had been like this since the night they'd made love— her body betraying her every attempt to restore the normalcy of their relationship.

"What's up?" Despite the racing of her own heart, she managed to speak casually.

"Is this a bad time?" he asked.

"I am in the middle of something," she said, although for the life of her she couldn't remember what it was. Something about the sound of his voice stirred up the unforgettable memory of its soft whisper against her ear as they'd made love and banished everything else from her mind. Yeah, sleeping with the man who was her best friend had been a very big mistake.

"Then I won't keep you," he promised. "I was just calling to see if you were free for dinner tonight."

"Actually, I'm not," she said. "I took a couple of hours off this afternoon to run some errands and need to stay late to catch up."

"You still have to eat," he reminded her.

"I'll pick up something on my way home."

"What time will that be?"

"I don't know."

His voice dropped. "I'd really like to see you tonight."

"I'm not going to marry you, Craig."

"So you keep saying." She could almost hear the smile in his voice. "I'd still like to see you tonight."

She didn't allow herself to hesitate; she couldn't afford to waver. "No."

"Are you afraid you might change your mind?"

"No," she said again, although they both knew she was lying.

"How about tomorrow, then?"

She sighed, uncertain how long she could hold out against his persistence. "Maybe."

Tess should have known that Craig wouldn't be appeased with a *maybe* and that he wouldn't wait until the next day. It was about six-thirty when he showed up at the office carrying a large paper bag and two crystal wineglasses.

"Since you couldn't go to dinner, I brought dinner to you," Craig told her, already unpacking the contents of the paper bag.

She wanted to send him away, to insist that she had work to do. But her stomach growled loudly as the scents of tangy tomato sauce and sweet basil tickled her nostrils.

"Chicken parm and spaghetti." He opened the lid and set the container in front of her.

How was she supposed to hold out against a man who knew all her weaknesses? It wasn't fair. She pushed aside her notes and picked up a plastic fork.

"I was going to get something to eat on the way home," she reminded him.

"I just wanted to make sure you had a proper meal."

Of course—this wasn't really about her, it was Craig's way of making sure she was taking care of the baby. Her suspicions were confirmed when he reached into the bag and pulled out a carton of milk. He filled the two wineglasses, handed one across the desk to her.

"I thought white was appropriate, since we're having white meat," he explained. "This is a domestic vintage, light-bodied, fresh, pleasing to the palate with a lingering finish."

As much as she wanted to resent his heavy-handed manner, she was helpless to resist his charm.

Craig held up his glass, tapped the rim against hers. "To date number two."

"This isn't a date," Tess said.

Craig merely smiled and sipped his milk.

"I'm not dating you," she insisted.

His smile widened. "I think two dates could be called dating."

"Saturday night wasn't a date, either."

"Oh." His brow furrowed as he considered her statement. "But we went to a movie together…shared popcorn…and a kiss good-night."

"That wasn't a kiss," she said, dismissing the moment when they'd stood outside her door and he'd brushed his lips against her cheek.

She'd been surprised when he'd parked instead of dropping her off at the front door as he would have done in the past. And with every step they'd taken up to her apartment, her anticipation had mounted so that by the time they reached her door her pulse was racing and her skin was flushed—and not from the physical exertion of walking the three flights of stairs.

She'd wanted him to kiss her, but she couldn't help remembering what had happened the last time, how quickly a kiss had turned into so much more. And though her body ached with wanting the so much more, she knew she couldn't fall into bed with Craig again with everything still unresolved between them.

As it turned out, she'd fallen into bed alone and had

lain awake late into the night, thinking about that kiss—the sizzle of awareness, the breathless anticipation and the undeniable disappointment when his lips brushed against her cheek. It was just like so many kisses they'd shared before—gentle and fleeting, over before it had begun without any hint of wanting something more.

"It was so a kiss," he said, managing to sound insulted that she'd implied otherwise.

"Not a date kiss."

He glanced up as he twirled his fork in the pasta, frowning with what was obviously feigned confusion. "What's the criteria for a date kiss?"

She shook her head, realizing too late the dangers of engaging in this type of conversation with a man who could heat her blood with a look, send her hormones rocketing with a casual touch and—God help her—make all of her reservations melt with a simple kiss.

"Come on, Tess. Help me out here."

As if he needed any help. The man had probably been on more dates in the past six months than she'd experienced in her lifetime. Besides which, she knew from firsthand experience that he didn't need any advice or guidance in the kissing department.

"I hate to think that I left you—" he paused, as if searching for the right word "—dissatisfied."

"I wasn't. You didn't." She shoved a forkful of pasta in her mouth and willed the heat to fade from her cheeks.

"I could try again," he suggested.

"Not necessary," she said. "Because that night was *not* a date. This is *not* a date. I'm *not* dating you and I'm *definitely not* going to marry you."

"I'm pretty sure it was a date," he said, pointedly ignoring the rest of her protest.

"We've been going to the movies together for years," she reminded him.

He tilted his head, considering. "If we've been dating for years, it shouldn't surprise you that I want to marry you."

She wouldn't let herself smile. She wouldn't admit that his charm and perseverance were effectively chipping away at her resistance. She had to stay strong—or at least fake it.

She sliced through the chicken breast with a plastic knife as she debated telling him about the two appointments she'd had today: one with Dr. Bowen, an OB-GYN, another with Jessica Armstrong, an attorney.

Since she was hungry and didn't want to fight with Craig anymore before she'd eaten her dinner she decided to tell him about her visit to Dr. Bowen first.

"I had a prenatal checkup today," she told him.

"How was it?"

"Good. It was just a routine first appointment. She put me on prenatal vitamins, told me to eat healthy and exercise and scheduled me for a follow-up next month."

"Can I come?"

"If you want," she agreed.

"I do."

Tess exhaled. Okay, maybe they *could* do this. As long as they could avoid the issues of marriage and sex, maybe they could just be two friends who were having a baby together.

The thought eased some of the pressure that had been building up inside her and they finished their meals in comfortable silence. She decided, in the interest of keeping the peace, that she would save telling him about the lawyer until another day.

When they were finished eating Craig emptied the last of the milk into Tess's glass. She'd already had two glasses, but she dutifully downed the third knowing it was good for the baby and would make him happy. And she was grateful they seemed to have taken a step toward resuming the easy camaraderie they'd once shared.

As she finished the milk, Craig gathered up the take-out containers, stuffed them back into the paper bag.

"Thanks for dinner," she said.

He smiled. "My pleasure."

She turned her attention back to the papers that were on her desk, waiting for him to leave. She reread the same paragraph three times before she gave in and glanced up at Craig, still standing beside her. "I thought you were going."

"I'm waiting for my good-night kiss," he said.

"You're going to be waiting a while."

"Come on, Tess. You can show me a proper date kiss."

"This wasn't a date," she reminded him.

"You know, it would help repair my sorely damaged ego if you at least pretended to be interested," Craig said.

"I don't think I've damaged your ego," Tess said dryly. "I don't think it's possible. Your ego's as rock-hard as your head."

"Ouch. Now that did hurt."

Tess laughed. "Go home, Craig."

He grinned at her and bent to touch his lips to her forehead. "Good night, Tess."

* * *

It was Thursday and Tess was becoming increasingly discouraged by her inability to track down either Owen or Carl. Every time she tried to catch one of them, he was on the phone or in a meeting or out of the office. And now, the receptionist told her, they were both out of town.

While Tess was frustrated by this latest obstacle, she was more unnerved when Elaine revealed where they'd gone: San Diego. Because she'd finally got around to doing some Internet research on Jared McCabe and learned why his name had been familiar to her. He was the President and CEO of GigaPix, a company she'd applied to right out of college, and a competitor of SBG.

While Tess wanted to talk to Owen and Carl before assuming the worst, she couldn't help but think the future of SBG was in question—and her job along with it.

This thought was weighing heavily on her mind when she got home from work that night. She kicked off her shoes inside the door and shuffled through the mail that she'd picked up downstairs. Telephone bill, credit card application, advertisement from a local pizza place and an envelope embossed with the names Huntington & Whitmore, Attorneys at Law and a return address in New York City.

Tess put the other mail aside and frowned at the letter from the lawyer. Not her lawyer, but a firm from the big city.

Craig's lawyer?

Her stomach plummeted at the thought as she slid a shaking finger beneath the edge of the flap and tore it open.

Re: 40 Centennial Drive

Her anxiety gave way to confusion and she quickly scanned the contents of the letter.

Her apartment building was being sold and this was her notice to vacate by the end of October. She reread it three more times before the reality sank in. Now she was pregnant and unmarried, potentially unemployed and soon-to-be homeless.

Then Tess did something she hardly ever did—she sat down and cried.

Chapter Six

Craig was at Tess's apartment less than thirty minutes after they got off the phone.

"What are you doing here?" she asked when she answered the door.

"You sounded like you could use a friend," he said, and he held up the pint of ice cream in his hand. "So I brought two of them—Ben and Jerry."

She managed a wan smile and stepped away from the door so he could enter. "You know me so well."

"Well enough to know that everything's not always fine just because you say it is." He went straight to the kitchen, found a spoon in the drawer and handed it to her along with one of the pints.

"I was overreacting," she said, prying the lid off the ice cream.

"You don't usually overreact."

"I try not to. I guess I was just feeling a little out of sorts when I got home and then I found the letter."

Craig followed her into the living room, took the envelope she handed to him. He read the contents while she dug into the ice cream.

When he was finished, he sat beside her on the sofa. "I'm sorry, Tess. I know how much you love this place."

"It's just an apartment," she said. "Logically, I know that. But I've lived here since I moved back to Pine-hurst. I know the neighborhood and the neighbors. I have a second bedroom that I was planning on making into a nursery."

"So you'll move to a new neighborhood and meet new neighbors," he said gently.

"I know." She offered him a spoonful of ice cream, which he declined with a shake of his head. "It's just one more thing that I wasn't prepared to deal with right now."

"You don't have to deal with it right now," he told her. "You have a couple of months to decide what you want to do, to make a list of desirable locations and the best schools and nearby parks."

"You're never going to forget that list, are you?" She shoved another spoonful of Chunky Monkey into her mouth.

He grinned. "Probably not."

"I like to know that I'm making the right decision for the right reasons," she admitted.

"That's why I know you'll figure this out," he said.

She sighed. "How is it that you always know exactly what to say to make me feel better?"

"It's a gift."

"It is." She put the lid back on the container and took

the leftover ice cream to the freezer. When she came back, she sat down next to him again. "And as much as I appreciate the ice cream, I'm even more grateful for your friendship."

He tucked his arm around her shoulders, drew her close. "I'll always be there for you, Tess."

She snuggled against him, laid her head on his chest. "I'm so afraid of losing you," she admitted softly.

"That's never going to happen," he said, then added, teasingly, "Of course, if you really wanted to be sure not to lose me, you could marry me."

She sighed, a release of breath that seemed to come from deep within. "I don't know why I thought we might actually have a whole conversation without the M-word."

"Wishful thinking," he told her, his hand moving in gentle circles over her back.

"Apparently." She stifled a yawn.

"I just want to make sure you don't forget my offer."

"I don't think that's likely."

"I could have it written into our vows that there would always be Chunky Monkey in the freezer," he offered.

"Tempting," she said. "But no."

He could feel the tension slowly seeping out of her as he continued to rub her back. And though his body was painfully aware of the softness of her curves nestled against him, he found himself enjoying the quiet comfort of the moment. There had been so much dissension between them lately, but he was glad that he could be here for her now.

After only a few minutes, Tess was asleep.

He wasn't surprised that she was tired. She was always on the go, always rushing from one thing to the next. She didn't seem to realize how much energy she was using just growing their baby inside her.

He knew, because he'd been doing a lot of reading on the subject. He'd bought a couple of books and had done some research online. It was amazing what could be found on the Internet—although he could gladly have done without the live birth videos he'd found himself watching. At first he'd been fascinated by the process, captivated by the miracle of birth. Until he'd superimposed Tess's image over the panting and obviously pained woman. Then, he'd been terrified.

He knew childbirth was a natural process, that women had been having babies for thousands of years—and most of those without the aid of modern technology. But even today, there could be complications and the thought of anything happening to Tess terrified him.

Of course, there was no going back now.

All he could do was stay by her side. Even if she wouldn't marry him—and he hadn't entirely given up on that idea yet—he would be with her through every step of this pregnancy, through labor and childbirth. And for the eighteen years after that, if she would let him.

Laurie responded to Tess's knock on the door Saturday morning with Devin propped on her hip and the shoulder of her blouse stained with spit-up milk. Her hair was mussed as though she'd repeatedly run her fingers through it—or had tried to pull it out by the roots—and her eyes filled with weary desperation.

The joys of motherhood, Tess thought.

But her sister managed a smile and held out the baby. "Can you take him while I get Becca ready?"

"Sure." Tess dropped her purse by her shoes and took Devin in her arms. "Is everything okay?"

Laurie nodded. "The kids are just fussing because they miss their daddy. Becca usually loves her swimming lessons but today she's parked in front of the television and refusing to get dressed and Devin hasn't let me put him down all morning."

"How long has Dave been gone?"

"Since Wednesday." There was a world of suffering in her response. "But he's coming home tomorrow."

She ducked into the living room and turned off the television. Becca howled in protest.

"You can't go swimming in your pajamas," Laurie told her daughter.

"Don't wanna go swimming." Becca crossed her arms over her chest and stuck out her bottom lip.

"If you don't go swimming, you won't get to see Kelly and Rachel."

"Don't wanna go swimming," Becca repeated.

Laurie sighed and rolled her eyes at Tess. "I'm just going to change my shirt, then I'll see if I can wrestle little miss pouty into her bathing suit."

Fifteen minutes later, Laurie had her daughter by the hand and was ready to head out the door. "He should be okay until I get back, but there's a bottle of expressed milk in the fridge if he starts to fuss. And drops," she pointed to a vial on the counter "to give him after his bottle. He's got a touch of colic and the medication seems to help."

"Colic?" Tess was sure she'd heard of it, but she had no idea what it was.

Laurie nodded. "It's basically gas. I give him some

drops when he nurses but he still cries all the time. The doctor said there's nothing really I can do and it's okay to just let him cry—but I can't stand to hear him so upset."

"Gotta go swimming, Mommy." Becca tugged impatiently on her mother's hand.

"Are you sure you're going to be okay?" Laurie asked her.

"I'll be fine." She ushered her sister out the door. "You just worry about Becca's swimming lessons."

"We'll be back in a couple of hours."

"Go."

Tess shut the door and smiled at her nephew. "Well, it looks like it's just you and me, kid."

Devin's answering smile wobbled, his lower lip jutted out and his eyes suddenly filled with tears.

An hour and a half later, Tess wondered why she'd ever thought she was cut out to be a mother. She'd fed Devin half his bottle and given him drops. She'd changed him, rocked him, paced with him and he still continued to fret and whimper. By the time Laurie and Becca returned, Tess was almost ready to sit down and cry right along with him.

"What's the matter, little guy?" Laurie passed off a takeout bag to Tess in exchange for the baby. Almost immediately, Devin's sobs subsided into soft hiccuping sounds. He rubbed his face against his mother's shirt, stuffed his thumb into his mouth and closed his eyes.

"Did he give you a hard time?" Laurie asked, rubbing her hand in circles against his back.

"Let's just say I now know what the expression 'trial by fire' really means."

"I'm sorry."

Tess shrugged. "I just felt so helpless. Nothing I did seemed to soothe him." She looked at him now, peaceful and content in his mother's arms. "I guess he just wanted his mommy."

"He has those moods," Laurie admitted. "And sometimes even mommy can't help."

"What do you do then?"

"Pass him off to Daddy. Devin likes to move around, so Dave usually takes turns walking the floor with him."

Which wouldn't be an option for Tess without a husband.

"Do you ever just let him cry?" she asked.

"I've tried," Laurie admitted. "But then Becca wakes up and I've got two cranky kids on my hands."

Tess peeked at the now sleeping baby and wondered how it was that such a tiny person had so much control over the adults in his life.

"Can you get Becca into her booster seat while I put Devin down for a nap?" Laurie asked.

Tess managed that task more easily and handed her niece the bag with the child's meal in it.

Becca reached inside eagerly. "Toy." She pulled out her French fries, then the cheeseburger and then frowned into the empty bag. "Toy," she said again.

"You can have your toy after you eat your lunch," Laurie said as she came back into the kitchen. "It's the only way I can get her to eat sometimes," she confided.

"How did you learn all this stuff?" Tess asked. "Is there a Parenting 101 course?"

Her sister laughed. "You'll learn quickly enough when you have your own."

But Tess wasn't so sure. And after the difficult morning she'd spent with Devin she was even less convinced that she had what it took to raise a baby alone. So why was she determined to do this on her own when Craig was so obviously willing to share the responsibility?

"Tess?"

She glanced up, startled. "Sorry?"

"I just asked if you wanted some ketchup for your fries."

"No, thanks."

"Ket-chup, ket-chup," Becca demanded.

"Okay, honey." Laurie got up to get the ketchup and squirted a drop on her daughter's hamburger wrapper.

"Are you okay?" she asked Tess.

She smiled. "How could you tell I was having a panic attack?"

"Because I've been there. Although I have to admit, I don't think I would ever have considered doing it on my own."

"You think I'm crazy, don't you?"

"Certifiable," Laurie agreed.

"I just don't want to screw this up."

"This?" Laurie asked. "The baby—or your relationship with Craig?"

She popped a French fry in her mouth. "Both."

"Is he still pressuring you about marriage?"

"Not directly."

"What does that mean?"

She felt herself blushing. "He's decided to court me."

"Oh, Tess. That is so sweet."

"It's so annoying," Tess told her. "Every time I turn around, he's there. Taking me to dinner, sending me flowers, bringing me ice cream, calling just to say hi, taking me to dinner. He feeds me a lot."

Her sister laughed.

"All done," Becca said, holding up her empty hands.

Laurie used a napkin to remove the last traces of ketchup from her daughter's fingers and face then pulled a plastic wrapped toy out of her pocket.

"Toy?" Becca said.

"Yes, toy."

"Mommy, open."

"Okay, honey." Laurie tore open the plastic, removed the miniature blue dog.

"Doggie," Becca said, dancing away happily with her new toy.

"It sounds like he's making a real effort," Laurie said. "How is it that you're still resisting him?"

"It's not easy," she admitted. And it wasn't. Craig had been so wonderfully attentive and supportive and she knew he'd be a great father.

"Then what's holding you back?" her sister asked.

Tess sighed. "I'm not sure I even know anymore."

Two months after he'd first proposed and despite repeated rejections of numerous subsequent proposals, Craig was still trying to figure out a way to convince Tess to marry him.

He refused to be frustrated by her refusals. He truly believed that marriage was the best solution to their situation and he was confident that Tess would realize it, too. Probably. Maybe. Eventually.

But it wasn't in his nature to sit back and wait for something he wanted, and he'd never wanted anything as much as he wanted to give his baby a family. Maybe he was old-fashioned. Maybe his image of family—a mother and father married to one another, raising their children together—wasn't the norm anymore. But it was what he'd longed for desperately growing up and it was what he wanted for his child.

He didn't ever want his son or daughter to have to answer the kinds of questions he'd been subjected to. Children weren't deliberately cruel, just innately curious, and he'd soon grown accustomed to inquiries about the mother who wasn't around. And he'd learned to feign indifference, refusing to let anyone see how much it hurt that his mother had walked out—that she hadn't cared about him enough to take him with her.

Not that he'd wanted to go, but why didn't she want to take him? He sometimes imagined that the letter she'd supposedly left was a forgery, that she'd really been kidnapped, torn out of his life against his will. Or that she'd gone willingly but only because she'd been suffering from some horrible illness and chosen to disappear from his life so he wouldn't have to watch her die. But despite the elaborate fantasies woven in his child's mind, his heart had always known the truth—she just didn't want to stay, she didn't want to be his mother, she didn't love him enough.

Tess's pregnancy might have been an accident, but it wasn't a mistake. Although he might not have planned on becoming a father at this point in his life, he wasn't going to shirk his duties or responsibilities. Yeah, there had been a moment—even several moments—of sheer panic and terror when he'd first faced the possibility that Tess could be pregnant with his child. But along with the acceptance had come an increasing sense of awe and anticipation and the startling realization that he loved this baby already. And he wouldn't give his child cause to doubt it.

Unfortunately, he was going to need something more than his own conviction and determination to sway Tess toward marriage. But what?

He picked up his beer and took a long swallow from the bottle, certain that if he thought long and hard enough, the answer to that question would come.

There wasn't anyone he knew as well as he knew Tess and he was sure there wasn't anyone who knew her as well as he did. Her favorite color was yellow, her lucky number twenty-two and she was addicted to home renovation and decorating shows. Her CD collection contained everything from opera to Ozzy; she read Patricia Cornwell novels and loved Disney movies. She enjoyed skiing but didn't know how to skate, adored dogs and was allergic to cats. She liked green apples and red grapes, drank her coffee black and ate her eggs scrambled. She was obsessive about punctuality and completely devoted to her family. He knew all this and more, but he didn't know how to convince her that a marriage between them would work.

He'd considered, but immediately rejected, the strategies he might use with any other woman. Tess wasn't the type to fall for any kind of grand romantic gesture and he knew that whisking her away for a weekend in Paris would more likely lead to apprehension than acquiescence.

"I didn't expect to be swept off my feet," she'd told him when he'd expressed doubts about her engagement to Roger. *"I don't* want *to be swept off my feet."*

He frowned, remembering their conversation, searching within it for a key to unlocking the barriers she'd put between them.

"What do you want?"

"I want to be with someone who wants to be with me. To share a home with him, raise a family together."

He scowled as he tipped his bottle to his lips again. He'd been sorry, for Tess's sake, that things hadn't worked out the way she'd hoped with Roger. But he'd also been relieved. He'd never thought the man was good enough for her and Roger's infidelity only proved how unworthy—and stupid—he was.

As Craig pushed himself off of the couch to head to the kitchen for another beer, he banged his shin on the corner of the glass coffee table. Damn, that thing was dangerous. Too dangerous to keep with a child toddling around.

Not that the baby would be toddling for quite some time, but his throbbing leg was a painful reminder that he'd need to do some serious childproofing of his home before that eventuality. Except that when he tried to picture a baby crawling on the antique Persian carpet, the image wouldn't come.

He twisted the cap off another bottle as he mentally rearranged furniture to make room for a crib and play-pen and all the other paraphernalia that went along with a baby and he realized that it just couldn't be done. His condo simply wasn't big enough for him and Tess and their child.

Okay, maybe he was jumping ahead a little, putting Tess into the picture, too, but he couldn't imagine making a home for their baby that didn't have her in it.

Because she was the mother of his child, he assured himself. Not for any other reason.

Except whenever he thought of Tess now, it wasn't always about the baby growing inside her womb. In fact, the image that most often came to mind was of Tess in his bed, naked and soft, her hair spread out on his pillow, her lips—swollen from his kisses—curved with satisfaction. It was the same picture that haunted his dreams and he would wake up yearning, reaching for her.

They'd been friends for fifteen years. Good friends. Best friends. And in all those years, he'd never considered breaching the boundaries of that relationship. Okay, maybe that wasn't entirely true. There was that one time—he'd just come home after his first year of college—when he'd realized the skinny awkward girl he'd said goodbye to in September had suddenly blossomed into a woman—a beautiful, desirable woman. But he'd ignored the immediate stir of interest, reminding himself that she was Tess—just Tess. His friend, his confidante.

Now suddenly, the woman who'd been "just Tess" for so many years was so much more. Except that she was brandishing their friendship like a shield against the possibility of any deeper relationship, and he was faced with the formidable task of having to convince her the status quo wasn't enough anymore.

But as he sat down to nurse his beer and his shin, he thought he might finally have an idea about how he might do just that.

Tess left for the office even earlier than usual Monday morning. She didn't know if Owen and Carl were back from their trip yet, but if they were, she was determined to catch them before anyone else showed up at work.

As it turned out, they were both waiting in her office when she walked in.

"Good morning," she said, forcing a nonchalance she didn't feel.

"Good morning," they both echoed her greeting.

She set her cup of coffee carefully on her desk and sank into her chair. "What's going on with GigaPix?" she asked.

"I told you she suspected there would be changes coming," Owen told his partner.

Tess tried to take comfort in his use of the word *changes* rather than *unemployment*.

"I hope you haven't been worrying yourself about this," he said to Tess.

"I'd rather plan than worry," she said, although she'd been doing a lot of the latter anyway. And though her pregnancy and the uncertainty of her relationship with Craig were the foremost concerns in her mind, the possibility of losing her job was a very close second.

She loved her job as an animation software programmer and though she was confident she would find other work to ensure she was taking home a paycheck, she knew there wouldn't be the same kind of opportunities she'd had at SBG because there weren't any other software companies in Pinehurst.

"That's good," Carl said. "Because no final decision has been made as of yet."

"But you're thinking of selling out to GigaPix," she guessed.

He nodded. "Jared has big plans for our programs

and with a staff twice the size of ours, I have no doubt he can implement them. But he's also agreed, for the sake of continuity and as a gesture of goodwill, to hire some of our programmers to continue working with the SBG programs. You're one of the programmers that we've recommended and Jared has agreed that he'd like to make you an offer."

The fear that had been building inside, verging on panic, finally started to dissipate.

Carl smiled. "You look a little surprised."

"I am," she said. "More than a little. When I saw both of you in here, I thought you were going to tell me that I was losing my job."

"On the contrary, if everything works out, this will be a heck of a promotion for you, Tess."

She wasn't just relieved, she was elated. A promotion was more than recognition of the work she'd done, it was an acknowledgment that she was capable of so much more. "When will you know for sure?"

"It will probably take a few more weeks to get all the details worked out," Owen said. "Once everything is ready to go, Jared will come back to speak with you himself, but we wanted to give you a heads-up."

"Thank you," she said. "Both of you, for recommending me."

"No thanks required," Carl told her.

"You've earned this," Owen added. "And you deserve it."

She wanted to laugh and shout and jump in the air, but she managed to limit herself to a smile as the two men rose to their feet.

"Just one question," Owen said, pausing at the

door. "How did you make the connection between Jared and GigaPix?"

"His name triggered something," she admitted. "So I did an Internet search and found out who he was. I actually applied for a job at GigaPix when I was finishing up at DeVry, thinking that I'd like to live in California, but I got an offer in Arizona first, then I came back here."

Owen smiled. "Looks like you'll get that chance to work at GigaPix and live in California after all."

She kept the smile on her face until her bosses had left her office, then buried her face in her hands as excitement and despair battled inside her.

California.

She'd assumed—wrongly, it turned out—that she would continue to work here. It hadn't occurred to her that Jared would move SBG across the country. Of course it made sense that he would, she just hadn't thought that far ahead. And it was still a tremendous opportunity for her, she knew it was. The Golden State. Her dream job.

There was just one problem: it would take her almost three thousand miles away from her baby's father.

Chapter Seven

Tess felt a quick surge of apprehension when she pulled into the parking lot of her apartment building and recognized Craig's Lexus in one of the visitor spaces. He was waiting on the front step for her this time and smiled when he saw her coming up the walk. He didn't wait for her to approach him, but met her halfway, taking her arm and steering her back toward the parking lot again.

"Craig, I'm just getting home. What are you doing?"

"There's somewhere I want to take you."

"Can't it wait?"

"Actually no, it can't."

She heard the excitement in his voice and decided she didn't want to dim his enthusiasm with talk of moving across the country. So she followed him back to his car, settled herself in the passenger seat.

She didn't ask where they were going but watched

the scenery outside her window and noted that they were moving north, in the direction that Craig lived. But when he drove past the exit for his condominium complex, she was baffled. Even more so when he turned into a long drive that led toward a two-story saltbox style home.

"Do you know the people who live here?" she asked cautiously.

"No," he said.

He pulled up alongside a red minivan that was already parked in the driveway. "Good, Tina's already here."

"Who's Tina?"

"The real estate agent."

He went around to open her door, but she remained immobile, not even unclipping her seat belt.

"What are we doing here, Craig?"

"Looking at the house."

"Why?"

"Because you have to move out of your apartment soon and there isn't enough room for you and me and the baby in mine."

She glanced wistfully at the house, then shook her head. "You know I can't afford to buy a house. Especially not a house like this." Especially not now.

She'd spent the first couple of years after college paying back her student loans. The savings and investments she'd so carefully compiled over the last few years might have made a nice little down-payment, but not on a house like this. And not when she would be moving to another state when GigaPix took over SBG. Because she knew that moving to San Diego was the logical thing to do, even if she wished, for personal reasons, that it wasn't a move she had to make right now. But it was the best thing for her career. Sure, she could probably find another job in Pinehurst, but nothing comparable to the position at SBG. And if she was going to support her baby, she needed to work.

Craig reached across to unfasten the belt for her. "There's no harm in taking a look."

"I just think it's a waste of time—yours, mine and the real estate agent's," she said, but she finally climbed out of the car.

"I'm glad to see you were running a little behind schedule, too," Tina called out the apology as she was unbuckling her baby from the back seat. "My usual after-hours sitter is sick and my husband was stuck in a late meeting at the office, so I had to bring Chloe for the tour."

"Not a problem," Craig told her, easily lifting baby Chloe from her mother's arms. "A beautiful woman—no matter how young—is always welcome."

Tina laughed. "That's the one thing I remembered about you, Craig—always a charmer." She hefted the diaper bag and briefcase onto her shoulder, then turned to offer her hand. "You must be Tess."

Tess shook her hand. "It's nice to meet you."

"I'm glad you were able to make it this afternoon," Tina said, already moving up the flagstone walk toward the front door. "This property was only listed two days ago, but there have been at least half a dozen couples to look at it already and I received a page while I was on my way here that there's an offer expected to come in on it tonight."

"That's fast," Craig commented.

Tina shrugged as she inserted a key into the lock. "Everything moves fast in this neighborhood."

Tess followed Craig, who still had Chloe in his arms, more fascinated by the comfort he displayed with the baby than by the gleaming hardwood floors and wide center staircase.

"We'll start the tour in the master suite," Tina said, leading the way.

It didn't take Tess long to realize why she'd started there. The room had a two-sided fireplace that divided the sleeping area from a sitting area, French doors that led to a private balcony and an ensuite bathroom with a separate shower and soaker tub and a skylight overhead.

"What do you think?" Craig asked.

"I think this room is almost bigger than my whole apartment."

"Probably," he admitted. "But what I really like is that there's enough room in the sitting area for a crib and change table and rocking chair."

Looking at Craig, standing in the center of the room with the baby tucked comfortably against his shoulder, Tess could picture it, too. It was almost too easy to imagine living in this house with him, sharing this room—and a bed—with him, raising their child together. She turned away, ignoring the ache that pierced deep into her heart, and followed Tina into the next room.

There were five other bedrooms and three more bathrooms on the upper level, then a den, formal living room, huge family room, another bathroom, dining room and kitchen on the main level. The kitchen was a dream: maple cabinets, granite countertops and a huge island. Not that she was much of a cook—but she could still recognize and appreciate the potential. There were French doors off the eating area to a large patio that overlooked the spacious backyard. And in the backyard was a covered sandbox and a wooden climber/swing set.

Craig came to stand behind her, looking over her shoulder into the yard. "You like it?"

She turned around, saw Chloe was patting Craig's cheeks with her dimpled fists, clearly infatuated with the man who was carrying her in his strong arms.

"What's not to like? It's beautiful."

"It would be a great place to raise a child," he said.

Chloe clapped her hands together, signaling her agreement.

Tess smiled. "It would, but it's practically sold already. And even if it wasn't, it's way beyond my means. Heck, it's probably even beyond my dreams."

"It's not," he told her. "We could—"

"No." She interrupted quickly, before he could finish making the offer, before she could be tempted by it.

And she would be tempted, because she'd known from the moment she stepped inside the front door that she wanted this house. She wanted her baby to have a home with a yard and a swing set.

"Think about it, Tess. It could be ours. Yours and mine and our baby's."

She could only shake her head as she swallowed around the lump in her throat. She had to tell Craig that SBG was being sold, that she would soon be moving to California. But not here—not with the real estate agent hovering in the background—and not now.

Soon, she promised herself. Just not yet.

It was Friday and Craig was spending the night with a cold beer and ESPN. He'd declined an invitation from his brother to join Gage and some friends for drinks at Maxie's, a local drinking establishment that was popular for its selection of martinis and two-story dance floor. Although he wouldn't have minded spending time with Gage, he'd grown weary of the bar scene a long time ago. And Maxie's had never been one of his favorite places— even less so since the debacle with his ex-fiancée.

Lana had worked in marketing at Richmond Pharmaceuticals, although he'd never been introduced to her before the night they'd crossed paths at Maxie's. His eyes had met hers across the bar and she'd smiled and started toward him. He found out later that she'd known exactly who he was before she ever came over to introduce herself.

They were engaged less than a year later and then Lana pressed for a short engagement insisting that she was eager to become Mrs. Craig Richmond and start their life together. It hadn't taken him long to realize that she was even more eager to start spending his money.

She'd asked for a temporary leave of absence from work so she could concentrate on planning their wedding, which included trips to New York City with her girlfriends to look for the perfect bridal gown, to search out the best master pastry chef to design their wedding cake, to find the most exclusive florist to import and arrange their flowers.

Craig had been startled by the cost of everything but he knew the wedding was important to Lana and he wanted her to be happy. It was a few months before their planned nuptials that he happened to come home early one day and overhear his fiancée admitting to her maid of honor that she had no intention of returning to her job in marketing. "I'll hardly need a pay-check from Richmond Pharmaceuticals when I'll have access to the entire Richmond fortune," she'd said matter-of-factly.

Craig had confronted her later that night, advising her not to waste the postage sending out invitations because there wasn't going to be a wedding. She'd sent them anyway, certain she could manipulate him into following through. He'd responded by personally calling each of the three hundred invited guests to advise that the wedding was off.

When her tears and pleas were similarly unsuccessful in changing his mind, she'd actually threatened to sue him for breach of promise. He'd dared her to try. She'd found someone richer—and more gullible—instead.

But that near miss had reminded Craig of the lessons he should have learned when his mother walked out of his life: when a woman said she loved him, his heart was going to take a beating. In his experience, women used emotions to camouflage their real motivations, and he'd been careful since his broken engagement to keep his relationships with women brief and uncomplicated. He made no promises and asked for none in return.

Until he'd proposed to Tess. But that was different. She was his friend—they liked and respected one another and wouldn't confuse their relationship with unwanted emotions.

Of course, he had yet to convince her to marry him.

Over the past several weeks, he'd managed to see her almost every day—either by stopping by her office or showing up at her apartment. If he didn't see her, he'd at least talk to her on the phone. He sent her flowers once a week and various other gifts: a new book by her favorite author, a cheesecake from her favorite bakery, a CD by her favorite jazz musician, an orange ceramic hippopotamus toothbrush holder because it was tacky and he knew she'd love it. Nothing too extravagant or pricey—just little tokens to let her know that he was thinking about her.

He took her to the theater, the flea market, a dog show. And although she was still insisting that she didn't want to marry him, he thought her protests were less adamant than they'd been at first and he was optimistic that eventually he would wear her down. Hopefully before their baby was born.

He glanced at the clock, considered calling her. But it was almost ten and when he'd spoken to her earlier that day, she'd told him that she was tired and planning an early night. When the phone beside him rang, he wondered if it might be Tess. But it was Nigel, the nighttime doorman, telling him that his brother was on his way up.

"I thought you were going to be at Maxie's tonight," he said, when he opened the door to let Gage into his condo.

"I was." Gage helped himself to a beer from the fridge, twisted the cap off, then dropped onto the sofa beside his brother and propped his feet up on the coffee table. "Then Debby showed up."

Craig picked up the remote and lowered the volume on the ball game. "Debby? The love of your life? The one who was going to ruin you for all other women?"

"Yeah, well, she tried," Gage muttered.

"What happened?"

"She started hinting—and none too subtly, either—that she expected a ring on her finger for our one-year anniversary."

"When would that be?" Craig asked, trying to remember when his brother had first mentioned the woman's name. It seemed to him it had only been a few months earlier.

"Valentine's Day," Gage said. "Six months from now."

Craig chuckled at the bafflement in his brother's voice.

Gage took a long pull from his bottle. "I'm twenty-seven years old. I have no interest in tying myself down to one woman at this point in my life—no matter how spectacular the sex is."

"Too much information."

His brother just grinned. "Speaking of information, there was another reason I wanted to stop by tonight."

"You mean there's a purpose to this visit other than to hide out where your girlfriend can't find you?"

"Yes," Gage said. "And it concerns your girlfriend."

Craig didn't know what to say. He knew Gage couldn't be talking about Tess—he couldn't know about the recent developments in their relationship—could he? And since Craig hadn't been dating anyone else in recent months, he was truly baffled by his brother's statement.

"Or rather, your ex-girlfriend," Gage said, which didn't clarify his statement for Craig at all.

"Karen?" he asked.

"Lana."

He found it a little disconcerting that his brother would bring up her name when she'd so recently been in his own thoughts. "What about her?" he asked.

"She was at Maxie's tonight."

That was even more surprising because he'd heard that she'd moved to Texas with her billionaire husband, Preston Sinclair.

"Dancing up a storm in a tight little dress that showed her God-given assets to full advantage."

"Not God-given," Craig told him.

"Well, you would know." His brother sighed with obvious disappointment. "And I should have guessed that they were too perfect to be real."

Just like the rest of her, Craig thought, but kept the comment to himself. Instead, he said, "And you should have realized Preston Sinclair wouldn't appreciate the way you were ogling his wife."

"Ex-wife," Gage said.

"They're divorced already?"

His brother nodded. "And Lana was making it clear to anyone and everyone that she's a single woman again."

Craig picked up his bottle, took a long swallow as he considered this revelation. He thought he should feel something but he really didn't care. Whatever feelings he'd had for Lana had been put to rest a long time ago.

"She made a point of talking to me," Gage continued. "Asking about you. I told her you were seeing somebody."

His brother was full of surprises tonight, although this was one Craig was grateful to hear. "Thanks."

Gage shrugged. "Hey, for all I know, you are seeing somebody. Just because your brother is always the last to know what's going on in your life…"

He ignored the not-so-subtle question along with any inclination to confide in his brother. Until he and

Tess figured out what they were going to do, he thought it was best to keep the news of her pregnancy quiet.

"If I ever feel the need to spill the details of my personal life, I'll let you know," he said instead.

"You'd have to actually have a personal life first," Gage pointed out.

Craig got up to get another couple of beers from the fridge.

"Does this mean you'll let me crash in your guest room tonight?" his brother asked, accepting one of the bottles.

"You can't hide out here forever," he said. "But for tonight—sure."

Craig wasn't surprised that Tess didn't respond immediately to his knock on the door Sunday morning. She'd always been a pretty sound sleeper and he knew she didn't believe in rising early on weekends, so he knocked harder and waited. He knew she was home because her car was in the parking lot downstairs and he'd just raised his hand to knock a third time when the door was pulled open.

"Are you trying to wake my neighbors, too?" she asked moodily.

Craig smiled and stepped past her into the apartment. "No, just you." He touched his lips to her cheek. "Good morning."

She raised a hand and pushed her tousled hair away from her face. Her eyes were still heavy-lidded from sleep, her face bare of makeup and her torso clad in an oversized, wrinkled T-shirt. She looked deliciously rumpled and incredibly tempting.

He'd always thought she was beautiful, just as he'd

always thought it was ridiculous to describe pregnant women as glowing. But there really was something different about her now, an indescribable something that simply took his breath away. And while there wasn't any obvious evidence of their baby growing inside her yet, he could already imagine how she would look when her belly was round with his child, and the mental image stirred within him both pride and possessiveness.

"What's so good about it?" she mumbled.

"You get to spend it with me," he told her.

She yawned. "Is there a second prize?"

"No." He turned to the kitchen. "Why don't you go get dressed while I make myself some coffee?"

"Because I didn't plan on getting dressed today," she said belligerently. "I want to stay in bed all day."

He grinned. "That sounds even better than what I had planned."

"Are you always this funny first thing in the morning?"

"Are you always this grumpy first thing in the morning?" he countered.

"Yes."

He measured coffee grounds into a paper filter. "If that's true, maybe I should rethink this whole marriage idea."

"You should definitely rethink it," she told him. "Because I am *not* going to marry you."

"You know, you don't sound quite as adamant as you did a couple weeks ago."

"I just need coffee. I can't argue coherently when my brain isn't even functioning."

She sat down at the table to wait for the coffee. As

she crossed one leg over the other, he couldn't help but notice that the oversized T-shirt she wore barely covered the tops of her thighs, displaying her long, slender legs to advantage. It was an effort to look away, to turn his attention to the cupboard where the mugs were located.

"Have you been cutting down on your caffeine intake?"

She glared at him. "I have one cup of coffee in the morning. The doctor has assured me that it won't harm the baby."

He poured coffee into a mug, added a generous amount of milk and passed it across the table to her.

"I take it black."

He grinned. "I know. The milk is for the baby."

"Has anyone ever told you that you're pushy and obnoxious?"

"Frequently," he admitted.

She sipped her coffee, grimaced.

"Do you want me to make breakfast or do you want to grab something to eat on the way?"

"On the way where?" she asked, her voice tinged with suspicion.

"It's a surprise."

"I've had enough surprises in my life lately."

"Well, today there's one more. Go get dressed."

Tess set her chin stubbornly. "I'm not going anywhere."

He sipped from his own mug. "I'd suggest you go and put some clothes on."

"Or what?"

The challenge in her voice was almost too much to resist. "Or I'll carry you to your bedroom and dress you myself." He allowed his eyes to skim over her boldly. "Or maybe just undress you. The choice is yours."

Her eyes dropped and she gulped down the rest of her coffee. "I'll get dressed."

He nodded. "Good idea."

Tess was stubbornly silent throughout most of the drive. It didn't take her long to figure out they were headed into New York City, but she didn't suspect why until she saw the approach for the George Washington Bridge. When she did, she was helpless to prevent the smile that curved her lips.

"We're going to Yankee Stadium?"

Craig chuckled and nodded.

"Why are you laughing?" she asked suspiciously.

"Because most of the women I know have a weakness for flowers or jewelry. Your weakness is baseball."

She shrugged. "It's just a different kind of diamond."

And it *was* her weakness, Tess admitted to herself as Craig sat back down beside her with the hot dogs he'd purchased at the refreshment stand. She loved the whole atmosphere of the ballpark: the bodies crammed shoulder-to-shoulder in the stands. Men, women and children, their faces glowing with excitement as the action played out on the field below. She breathed deeply, inhaling the scents of roasted peanuts and spilled beer, dry dust and fresh sweat.

"Are you having fun?" Craig asked, handing her a hot dog generously doctored with ketchup and mustard.

There was no way she could deny it, especially when her Yankees were winning.

"Yes, I am." She took a bite of her hot dog.

He grinned and handed her a napkin. "Good."

The crack of a bat echoed through the stadium and

the crowd rose as one to watch the ball soar high over the right field fence.

"Another two runs for the Yankees," Tess said proudly.

She was enjoying herself, more than she'd expected. She hadn't had many opportunities to relax lately and that Craig had not only known she needed such a diversion but provided it, reminded Tess how well he could read her. And how nice it was to have someone in her life that she could count on.

She took another bite of her hot dog as a voice inside her head nagged to remind her that he could be a permanent part of her life—her husband and a father to their baby.

Except that she didn't want to marry a man who didn't love her, who would never love her. And the one thing she knew about Craig was that he'd closed off his heart to the kind of happily-ever-after love she dreamed of sharing with a man someday. Just because she'd screwed up with Roger didn't mean she'd given up hope of finding the kind of once-in-a-lifetime love her parents had shared.

But maybe she needed to rethink her dreams now that she had a baby on the way. Maybe it was selfish to want more than what he was offering. Maybe she was being unrealistic in wanting the man she loved to love her back.

Her breath caught in her throat as panic ballooned inside her. Oh, no. No way. She nixed that thought immediately.

She was *not* in love with Craig!

He was her friend—her best friend. Other than Laurie, he was the only person in her life that she could really count on. Falling in love with him would be crazy.

She swallowed the last bite of hot dog, felt it slide

like lead into her stomach as she tried to reassure herself that she wasn't in love with her best friend. She was simply overreacting to the situation, dealing with the hormonal overload from her pregnancy. Yes, that made sense. Certainly more sense than that she'd fallen in love with her best friend.

What was love anyway?

She'd thought she'd been in love with Roger, but obviously she'd been wrong. She cared about Craig, that was only natural given their history and yes, she'd even go so far to say she loved him—as a friend. But anything more than that wasn't possible.

There should be some kind of test for love—a questionnaire, maybe. No less than three questions and if you didn't answer all questions positively, you weren't in love.

Question number one: Do you think of him at all hours of the day, even when your mind should be occupied with other tasks?

Question number two: Do you miss him when you're not with him and look forward to the next time you'll see him again?

Question number three: Can you imagine yourself spending the rest of your life with this person?

Tess mentally reviewed the list of questions and her answers. Yes…yes…and…yes.

Oh, God—she *was* in love with Craig.

"Tess?"

She glanced up, saw the concern in his dark brown eyes, in the crease between his brows.

"Sorry?"

"I asked if you wanted another hot dog."

She shook her head. "No. Thank you."

The crease between his brows deepened. "Are you okay? You seemed to go pale all of a sudden."

"I'm okay."

"Are you sure? Maybe it's the sun. Are you too hot?"

"I'm fine," she snapped.

"Okay." He still looked unconvinced but he let it drop.

Fine, she mocked herself.

How could she be fine when she'd just realized she was in love with her best friend?

Oh, she'd really made a mess of things now. She felt like she was standing at the plate, watching the balls scream past in quick succession before she even had a chance to swing the bat.

She'd had sex with Craig: strike one.

She was pregnant: strike two.

She'd fallen in love: strike three.

She was out.

Out of her mind—in love with her best friend.

Now what was she going to do?

Well, the one thing she was not going to do was tell Craig she'd made the colossal mistake of falling in love with him.

Because she knew how he'd react: he'd be shocked, then panicked, then he'd withdraw from her. Maybe not immediately and probably not obviously, but inevitably—because Craig didn't do messy emotions.

She'd been worried about how the revelation of her pregnancy would affect their friendship but that was nothing compared to *this*. Craig didn't trust love and he wouldn't trust her feelings if she was foolish enough to admit to them. He wouldn't believe she wasn't using the words for some ulterior purpose. Because he didn't

believe that anyone ever had or could love him uncon-
ditionally.

Tess knew otherwise, of course. His father—
although often preoccupied with the business—had
always been there for Craig. And Grace—Allan's
second wife—had fallen in love with both of her step-
children as quickly as she'd fallen for her husband.
But it was the withdrawal of affection from his natural
mother that had left such deep wounds, and though Tess
wanted to believe her love might be enough to heal
them, she couldn't be certain. And she wasn't ready to
face yet another rejection.

No, the one thing she knew for certain was that
she wasn't going to tell Craig about her newly discovered feelings.

The whole office was buzzing with the news that
SBG was being bought out by GigaPix and speculation
was rampant about the fate of SBG's employees. As
Tess strode briskly down the hall toward the conference
room for her meeting with Jared McCabe, she was
grateful the moment of truth, at least for her, had finally
arrived. She wiped her damp palms down the front of
her skirt before knocking on the door.

"Come in."

Tess did so, entering the room to face Jared McCabe
across the wide polished table. He offered his hand, as
he had the first time they met, then gestured for her to
be seated.

"As of October first, SBG will become a subsidi-
ary company of GigaPix Corporation and its opera-
tions will move to the corporate headquarters in

California. I'd like you to come to San Diego to be part of the GigaPix team." Then he opened one of the folders that were lined up in front of him and outlined the terms of his offer, including a salary that almost made her eyes pop out.

She should have been reaching for a pen, asking where to sign the contract of employment. Instead, she said, "It's a generous offer."

Jared closed the folder, his eyes narrowing speculatively on her.

She swallowed. "And I'm grateful for it. But…"

He waited silently.

She swallowed again, not quite believing the words that were coming out of her mouth. But she'd lain awake through most of the night thinking about so many things: her career, her pregnancy and overriding all else, the realization that she'd fallen in love with her baby's father. And she'd finally understood why she'd been unable to tell Craig about her intention to move to California—because she'd never really intended to go.

Sure, she'd entertained the idea, maybe even dreamed about the possibilities. But the reality was, she couldn't move three thousand miles away from her best friend, the father of her child, the man she loved.

"But I can't move to San Diego," she finished.

Now that Tess had made the decision to stay in Pinehurst, she was scrambling. She had until October thirtieth to find a new apartment but only until the first—less than two months away—to get a new job.

She was poring over the classified section of the newspaper when Craig stopped by her apartment Saturday morning with croissants and cappuccino. He took a seat across from her at the table completely covered with newspapers and watched her work.

She tried not to let his scrutiny distract her as she circled the apartment ads that sounded promising, then looked up the locations in her map book. She had a notepad beside her, where she was jotting down the addresses and making notes about the proximity to schools, parks and recreation centers.

She was waiting for him to make a crack about her "list" but he only said, "You're overthinking this, Tess. Just check out the places that sound good and go with what you like."

"I'm not overthinking it," she denied. "I'm trying to save myself time running around to places that are unsuitable."

He picked up one of the newspaper pages she'd scanned and set aside. "Here's one," he said, and began to read. "Rooms available for rent in a privately owned home overlooking green space in desirable Woodland Park neighborhood. Private bath and kitchen, huge backyard, plenty of parking."

"Let me see that." She grabbed the paper from his hand, frowning as she looked for—and failed to find—the listing. "You made that up."

"Well, I didn't want to actually advertise it in the paper. Imagine what kind of crazies might respond."

She pushed a hand through her hair. "Craig, I'm serious about this. I need to find a place so I can get settled in and ready for the baby."

"I'm serious, too. I want you to move in with me."

"But you don't have…" Her eyes widened. "Oh, my god—you bought the house?"

"Well, I've signed the papers," he said. "The deal doesn't officially close until next week."

She shook her head. "You're crazy."

"Actually, Tina assured me it was a wise investment."

"Is that why you bought it?"

"No," he admitted. "I bought it because I could picture our child sleeping in the nursery and playing in the backyard and then I couldn't imagine anyone else living there."

She felt her throat tighten with unexpected emotion.

"What do you think?" he asked. "Want to move in with me?"

She should say no firmly and finally. This idea was almost as crazy as marriage and yet she couldn't help but be tempted.

"There are plenty of bedrooms to choose from," he reminded her. "And then we could both be there full-time for our baby."

"Living together doesn't seem that different than getting married," she protested.

"I'm still open to marriage," he told her. "But I thought I should put this out there as an alternative."

No way. If she said yes to his offer she'd be as crazy as he was. But she did need somewhere to live and she did want her baby to have a father.

And she wanted to be with Craig.

She took a deep breath. "Okay."

"Okay?" He stared at her, clearly taken aback by

her sudden capitulation. "Is that an okay—you'll move in with me?"

She shook her head. "No, it's an okay—I'll marry you."

Chapter Eight

They were the words Craig had started to despair of ever hearing her speak. That she'd said them now left him completely speechless. At least for a moment.

"You really want to get married?" he asked cautiously, when he'd finally found his voice.

"Sure."

It wasn't quite the definitive response he would have liked, but it was an improvement on no. Still, he had to ask, "Why?"

"Do you want me to make a list of all the reasons I've changed my mind?"

"You mean you haven't already?"

"No." Her fingers curled around the pad of paper in her hand, gripping it so tightly her knuckles turned white. "It was an impulse—and one I'm already starting to question."

"Don't," he said quickly. "I don't know what caused this sudden change of heart but I really believe this is the right decision. I'm glad we're finally on the same page about what we want."

Tess didn't meet his gaze but stared instead at the list clutched in her hand.

"We are on the same page about what we want, aren't we?" he asked.

"I want my baby to have a family," she agreed, finally looking up at him. "And I can't think of anyone who would make a better father than you."

Her confidence bolstered his doubts and her willingness to take this leap of faith strengthened his determination to ensure she would never regret it. "Thank you."

He reached across the table to uncurl her fingers from the paper and link them with his own. "How soon do you think you can get away for a wedding and honeymoon?"

She seemed startled by his question. "You don't waste any time, do you?"

"Now that we've made the decision, I don't see any point in waiting."

"You're right," she agreed. "But a honeymoon isn't necessary. This isn't—"

He touched a finger to her lips, halting her protest. "Make no mistake about it, Tess, what I want is a real marriage and what I'm asking of you is a real commitment."

She swallowed. "I thought…"

"What did you think?"

"I thought you just wanted both of us to be there for our baby—to live separate lives under the same roof."

"Where would you ever get that idea?"

"From you," she said. "Not ten minutes ago. When you asked me to move in with you, you said there were a lot of bedrooms…"

"That was before you agreed to marry me," he pointed out.

She chewed on her bottom lip. "What exactly do you mean by a real marriage?"

He smiled. "I'm sure you can guess."

"You mean…one bedroom."

"I'm hoping," he admitted. "But that decision is yours."

"Oh." She exhaled and it sounded almost like a sigh of relief.

The unenthusiastic response immediately deflated his hopes. "Apparently you had a different idea."

"It's just that you haven't seemed…interested…in me. Lately."

He was stunned. "Why would you think that?"

"Well—" her cheeks flushed prettily "—you haven't even kissed me in weeks."

He hadn't done so deliberately, because he hadn't wanted to pressure her. But damn, it had been hard to keep his hands off her. "Not for lack of wanting," he assured her.

"Oh."

But he could tell by the furrow in her brow that she still didn't get it. And he knew he had to tell her the whole truth so that wherever they decided to go from here, that decision wouldn't be based on any kind of miscommunication.

"I haven't kissed you, Tess, partly because I didn't want you to accuse me of trying to seduce you into marriage, but mostly because I was afraid that if I started, I wouldn't want to stop."

"Oh," she said again, then, more softly, "I wouldn't want you to stop, either."

It took all of his willpower not to pull her into his arms and test her statement right then. But from the moment he'd found out she was pregnant, he'd tried to think about what was best for Tess and his baby rather than his own wants. And that meant getting married before they did anything else.

He took a step back, away from temptation. "Let's go shopping."

Tess stared at the dazzling collection of diamond engagement rings displayed on the burgundy velvet cloth. She felt completely overwhelmed—not just by the selection of rings but by everything that had happened in the past hour since she'd agreed to marry Craig. She was still trying to wrap her head around that impulsive decision and he was already planning the wedding.

Maybe she should be grateful—obviously someone had to take care of the details. But she hadn't thought beyond the moment and she didn't seem capable of making any more decisions right now. She couldn't even decide on a ring and they'd been in the jewelry store for at least thirty minutes already, tucked into a private office with Brian Shaw, manager of The Diamond Jubilee.

Craig laid his hand on her shoulder. "What do you think?"

She thought she was going to go blind if she kept staring at these rocks. "A simple gold band would be fine."

She saw a muscle in his jaw flex then relax. He turned to the jeweler. "Could we have a minute, Mr. Shaw?"

"Of course, Mr. Richmond."

He didn't say anything else until they heard the soft click of the door behind Mr. Shaw as he left the room. When he spoke, his voice was gentle, almost concerned. "I know this isn't going to be the wedding you always dreamed about, Tess, but I want to make it special for you."

"I just don't want you to feel obligated—"

"Tess," he interrupted.

She glanced up, hoping he wouldn't see the combination of excitement and uncertainty she felt reflected in her eyes. Desperately hoping he wouldn't suspect the unacknowledged and ever-growing feelings in her heart.

"I'm *very* happy you agreed to marry me," he said. "And I'd like to buy you an engagement ring as a token of my appreciation and affection. Do you have any objection to that?"

"No," she said, because any other response would sound ridiculous. And she didn't object, but she was disappointed. She wanted to be marrying Craig not just because she was pregnant with his child, but because he loved her as much as she loved him. "I'm sorry—I guess I'm just feeling a little overwhelmed because everything is happening so fast."

He smiled. "Maybe I don't want to give you a chance to change your mind."

She turned sideways in her chair so she could see his face. "What if you change yours?"

"After weeks of campaigning for you to marry me, why would I change my mind now?"

"Because now you know it's really going to happen—

we're going to get married and have a baby together and you're going to be stuck with both of us for the rest of your life."

"Are you trying to scare me?"

"Maybe."

"Then you'll have to try harder. I've thought about this from every angle, considered every alternative. The truth is, you're the only woman I can imagine spending the rest of my life with."

It wasn't a declaration of love, but it was an affirmation of his commitment to her and Tess knew she would have to be satisfied with that—at least for now. If he cared about her enough to marry her, she wanted to believe that someday he might fall in love with her, too.

In the meantime, he was anxious to put a ring on her finger and though Tess wanted to accommodate him, the vast selection of diamonds simply overwhelmed her.

He gestured to the collection spread out before them. "Is there anything you like?"

She looked them over again, hoping that something would catch her eye, but none did.

"They're all spectacular," she said, "but they're…"

Craig smiled when she paused. "What are you trying not to say? Gaudy? Tacky? Ostentatious?"

She still hesitated, thinking that any of those descriptions would fit. "They're just not me," she said at last.

He selected a ring at random—an enormous heart-shaped solitaire on a braided gold band—and slid it onto her finger. The diamond overwhelmed her slender hand so much that even Craig shook his head. He tried another ring—a pear-shaped diamond that weighed a ton—or at least several carats. "What do you think?"

She looked at him and raised her brows. "I wouldn't be able to go out in public without worrying that I'd be mugged."

He chuckled softly. "Okay, maybe we need to look at something different."

A brisk knock preceded Mr. Shaw's return a few minutes later. "Have we made any progress?" he asked.

Craig shook his head. "I think we're looking for something out of the ordinary."

"And a little more subtle," Tess added.

"A colored stone, perhaps?" Mr. Shaw asked. "We have a fabulous selection of Colombian emeralds and Indian sapphires."

Craig looked at Tess. She shrugged.

"Let's take a look at the sapphires," Craig suggested.

"I'll be right back," the manager promised, bundling up the unwanted diamonds before disappearing again.

"Why a sapphire?" Tess asked, hoping that he would give her a response that was more unique than some cheesy reference to the color of her eyes.

"Because it was believed by ancient civilizations that the world rested on top of a sapphire and that the color of the sky was a reflection of the stone." He picked up her hand, laced their fingers together. "You're giving me everything I want, Tess. In return, I want to give you the world."

From any other man, the explanation might have sounded scripted, but he spoke as if the words were really coming from his heart and she couldn't help but be touched by his sincerity.

Then she caught the twinkle in his eye just before he added, "And because a sapphire will match your eyes."

He grinned when she tugged her hand out of his grasp.

Before she could respond, Mr. Shaw returned, this time with a smaller, but still impressive, collection of rings that he laid out carefully on the velvet cloth.

Tess surveyed the selection, her gaze lingering on a modest square-cut sapphire flanked by graduated baguette diamonds. It was different and stunning, and obviously Craig thought so, too, because he immediately reached for it.

"Do you like it?" he asked Tess, watching closely as if to gauge her reaction.

"It's beautiful."

He smiled, apparently pleased that they'd finally found something they both liked. He took her hand and slid the circle of gold onto the third finger. It fit as if it had been made for her.

"That one's a Diamond Jubilee original. Designed by my daughter," Brian Shaw said proudly. "It's an eighteen-karat gold band with a one-carat Kashmir sapphire and six of the highest quality baguette diamonds."

"Is there a wedding band that goes with this?" Craig asked.

"No," the manager admitted. "But we can design one to match if you like."

"It will have to be ready by the middle of the week," he said.

"Of course, Mr. Richmond."

His response made Tess wonder, once again, if anyone actually succeeded in saying no to Craig. Lord knows she'd tried—she'd told him over and over again that she wasn't going to marry him. And now she was wearing his engagement ring on her finger.

Craig reached for Tess's hand as they left the jewelry store, rubbed his thumb over the ring on her finger. It was a symbol—solid, tangible proof that she would soon be his wife. He waited for the wave of terror to hit, was prepared to battle back the fear. He wasn't going to screw this up. He'd made a promise to Tess and he intended to keep it.

But as his finger stroked over the smooth band, he felt none of the expected panic. What he felt instead was satisfaction, happiness even. He frowned. Their marriage was a means to an end—his way of ensuring his place in his child's life. So why was he suddenly beginning to think that it could be so much more? Why was he thinking about the benefits of having Tess as his wife instead of just the mother of his child?

He continued to ponder these questions as they walked back to his car. "Did you want to grab a bite for dinner before I take you home?" he asked.

"Just because I'm pregnant doesn't mean you always have to be feeding me," she told him.

"Actually, my offer had nothing to do with your pregnancy and everything to do with the fact that I'm hungry and I thought you might be, too."

"I guess I am," she admitted.

"Are you in the mood for anything in particular?"

"Honey garlic chicken wings."

"Really?" He was surprised—Tess wasn't usually a big fan of chicken wings.

She shrugged "I seem to be having some unusual cravings lately."

"Like what?"

"Dill pickle potato chips. Coconut shrimp. Caesar salad."

"At the same time?"

She laughed. "No. Not so far, anyway."

"But tonight you want honey garlic chicken wings?"

"Yes."

"Okay, then, chicken wings it is."

They picked up a double order of honey garlic wings, fried rice and egg rolls and took it back to her apartment. Tess dug into the food with surprising appetite and no indication that she was still suffering from the nausea she'd complained about only a few weeks earlier.

"Have you had any more morning sickness?" he asked.

She gave a slight shake of her head as she licked sticky sauce from her fingers and he found his gaze riveted to the actions of her tongue, forgetting his own question until she responded, "The nausea seemed to pass after the first six weeks. Now the only problem I seem to have is controlling my appetite. I've already gained back the few pounds I lost in those early weeks and another four."

He let his eyes skim over her still slender form. He'd always thought she was a little too thin and though he really couldn't tell that she'd added a few pounds, he thought she looked great. Healthy. Glowing. And all the other clichés about pregnant women. "The extra pounds look good on you."

She dipped her egg roll into the plum sauce. "Let's see if you still think so in another six months."

"Let's see how much you really eat," he teased. "I need to know if I can afford to feed you for the next six months."

"Actually, that is something we should discuss."

He spooned some more rice onto his plate. "I was kidding, Tess."

"I know," she said. "But I don't expect you to be financially responsible for me."

"What does that mean?"

"I want to pay my own expenses."

He sighed wearily. "Tess, you're going to be my wife. For better or for worse; for richer or for poorer. I'm not going to start divvying up the household bills."

"Then I can buy the groceries."

"That's not necessary," he protested.

"Yes, it is. I need to make some kind of contribution."

"Fine," he relented, because he knew it was important to her even if he didn't really understand why. "You can buy the groceries."

"Thank you."

"Do you want to do the cooking, too?" he asked.

She dragged a chicken wing through the sauce in the bottom of the container. "Do you want to live on meat loaf and peanut butter sandwiches?"

"No," he admitted. "But I probably could live on your oatmeal chocolate chip cookies."

She smiled. "Cookies I can do."

He studied her thoughtfully. "How is it that someone who can bake like you do—" and she did make the best cakes and cookies and all other kinds of desserts "—can't master a simple pot roast?"

"Have you ever made a pot roast?" she challenged.

"No."

"Then how can you say it's simple?"

Okay, she had a point there. "You're going to insist on sharing kitchen duties, aren't you?"

"Unless you want to take on all the responsibility yourself," she told him.

"You know I'm not a great cook, either."

"But you're good with a barbecue."

"Maybe I should hire a housekeeper—someone who can appreciate the great kitchen we're going to have."

"Or maybe we should learn to cook."

"Hiring a housekeeper would be easier," he pointed out, as he started clearing their dishes from the table. "Someone to cook *and* clean."

And he would do it, Tess realized. Because he could afford it and it would make their life easier. But she didn't intend to take advantage of his offer.

"If you do the cooking, I'll do the cleanup," she said, trying to take the plates from him so she could load the dishwasher.

He nudged her gently aside and completed the task on his own. "I don't mind the cleanup and you shouldn't be putting your pretty hands in dishwater."

"Pretty hands?" she asked skeptically.

"Very pretty," he said, linking them with his own. "Especially now that you've got my ring on your finger—proof that you're going to marry me."

"You know the old saying—be careful what you wish for?"

He smiled. "I'm not worried."

But she was. She didn't usually make decisions impulsively—especially not decisions of this magnitude. True, she'd spent a lot of time over the past couple of weeks thinking about Craig's proposal and the reasons to accept or refuse. But she'd remained firm in her belief that marriage would be a mistake—until she realized she'd fallen in love with him, then all common sense had apparently deserted her. Or maybe she'd fallen in love because all common sense had already deserted her—it was the only explanation she could think of for loving a man who'd made it clear he didn't want any emotional entanglements.

"Maybe you should be worried," she said. "I know you didn't flinch at the four pounds but I'm going to gain at least twenty more over the next six months."

"Uh-huh." He reached out and laid a hand on the tiny bulge of her tummy. "I can't wait for your belly to grow round, for everyone to know it's my baby you're carrying."

His touch was gentle, his smile almost reverent and in that moment Tess knew that if she hadn't already been in love with him, she would have fallen right then.

"You really are looking forward to being a daddy, aren't you?"

"The idea threw me for a loop at first," he admitted. "But yeah, I'm excited about having a baby with you and very glad that you finally agreed to marry me."

She was excited, too. And apprehensive. Because as much as she wanted to marry him and give their baby a family—she was worried that she would end up wanting more from their marriage than he could give her.

He took her hand again, held it up to gaze at the ring she was wearing. "You know, this makes it official."

She nodded.

"Which means that you have no reason to question my motives when I do this."

Then he kissed her.

And it was a real kiss this time. Lips on lips, soft yet firm but all too brief. His eyes stayed open, watching her as he kissed her again, lingering just a little longer this time.

She leaned forward, sliding her arms around his neck and instinctively pressing her body closer to his. Craig didn't need any more of an invitation.

His mouth covered hers again, his tongue gliding over the seam of her lips, dipping inside when they parted on a sigh of longing and her brain shut down completely.

She couldn't think, she couldn't reason, she could only feel. She felt her heart hammering against her ribs, her blood pulsing through her veins and the ground shifting beneath her feet.

He didn't try to deepen the kiss. He didn't touch her at all except with his lips. And never had she been so completely devastated by a kiss. She wasn't inexperienced, but she'd never experienced anything like this. She'd been kissed passionately, angrily, lustfully, but never so…tenderly. And it was his infinite patience and tenderness that arrowed straight to her heart.

When he finally eased his lips from hers, she was breathless and aching with wanting. And she knew that if he asked to stay she wouldn't say no because she wanted nothing more than to make love with the man she loved.

But he didn't ask.

He only said, "Good night, Tess." And then he walked out the door.

* * *

Craig wasn't sure how his parents would react to the news of his upcoming marriage but he did know that he couldn't imagine such a momentous event taking place without his family being present. So after confirming all the other details he made his way to his father's office.

He timed it so he'd arrive when Lorraine, his father's secretary, would be at lunch. That way, there wouldn't be any witnesses if his father started screaming. Not that his father ever really yelled but Craig had never dropped this kind of news in his lap before so he was prepared for almost anything.

Anything except finding his mother in a passionate lip-lock with his father when he walked through the door.

He immediately looked away, startled—though more pleased than embarrassed—to witness his parents kissing.

It amazed him that even after twenty years of marriage, they were still so obviously in love with one another. It was what he'd once wanted, too—an enduring connection with someone, a sense of belonging to that other person, a forever kind of love. But the closest he'd ever come to that feeling of unconditional acceptance was his friendship with Tess and that bolstered his conviction that their marriage, even though not based on love, would succeed.

"Sorry," he apologized quickly. "Your door was open."

"That's okay," Grace said, stepping out of her husband's arms. "I was just on my way out."

"Actually, I'd like you to stay for a few minutes, please. There's something I wanted to talk to both of you about."

"What's on your mind?" Allan asked.

Craig couldn't think of a way to ease into the topic, so he simply said, "Tess and I are getting married."

He noted the obvious surprise on both of their faces. Then his father frowned, his mother smiled.

"This is…unexpected," Allan said at last.

"The wedding's on Saturday at the Coral Beach Resort in Christ Church, Barbados. I know it's short notice, but I'd like you to be there if you can."

"Short notice?" Allan sputtered. "A month is short notice. This is less than a week and—"

"Of course we'll be there," Grace interrupted, laying her hand on her husband's arm.

His father closed his mouth, but the frown remained.

"Thank you," Craig said to his mother, already moving back toward the door. "Tess and I will be leaving on Friday and staying for a week, but you can make whatever arrangements suit you best."

"I'll call the airline today," she promised him.

He nodded. "I've got to get back to the lab."

And he backtracked out of his dad's office before they could inundate him with the questions he knew had to be racing through their minds.

Chapter Nine

Tess stood on the edge of the patio, waiting for her cue to head down the stone path toward the flower-covered archway on the beach where her groom was waiting. Only eight days had passed since she'd accepted Craig's proposal and today she would become his wife.

One hand clutched the bouquet of fresh, tropical flowers in her hands, crushing the delicate stems. The other pressed to her quivering stomach, willing her nerves to settle.

She caught a glimpse of her reflection in the window of the gift shop and almost didn't recognize the woman who looked back at her. Craig's preparations for the wedding had included The Ultimate Indulgence Package at the hotel spa and she'd spent the morning being scrubbed and buffed and polished, her hair swept into some fancy do on top of her head, her makeup artfully applied. He'd taken care of everything—all she had to do was walk down the aisle.

Her pulse began to race as the first notes of "The Wedding March" sounded. She'd never heard a calypso version of the song before, but it seemed appropriate for an island wedding.

Taking a deep breath, she put one foot in front of the other.

Since she was a young girl, she'd dreamed—as every young girl does—of getting married one day. But even in her wildest fantasies she'd never imagined that she'd find herself with a man like Craig Richmond. He was a real-life Prince Charming: kind, compassionate, giving—not to mention devastatingly gorgeous and sexy as sin. And he was going to be her husband.

And though she knew that he was only marrying her because of the baby, she really did love him and secretly vowed that she would do whatever she could to make him happy.

She turned the corner and saw Craig standing in front of a decorative arch set up under the palm trees on the beach. He was formally dressed in a dark suit and tie that had to be uncomfortable in the ninety-degree heat, but he looked cool and composed and so incredibly handsome her breath caught.

His eyes met hers and he smiled.

Only then did she realize that he wasn't alone. The minister was there, of course, but so was Craig's brother, Gage, and Grace and Allan. And on the other side of the minister stood Laurie and Becca, both holding smaller bouquets of flowers similar to her own.

Her eyes blurred with tears and her steps faltered, until

Craig stepped forward and held out his hand. And the last traces of nerves settled as she placed her hand in his.

She had little recollection of the actual ceremony. It all seemed to happen so fast and then the minister was pronouncing them husband and wife and inviting Craig to kiss the bride.

She expected a perfunctory wedding kiss. But when he lowered his head and brushed his mouth over hers, there was nothing casual or cursory about it and she felt her lips tremble in response. He lingered, drawing out the moment without deepening the kiss, and she tasted warmth and tenderness, heat and passion and so much more.

They had dinner with their families on a private terrace of the dining room and later, when they returned to their room, a bottle of chilled champagne and two crystal flute glasses awaited them along with a note of congratulations from the management and staff of the hotel.

"The honeymoon package," Craig explained.

"They think about everything, don't they?" She set the card back onto the table, suddenly nervous.

"You could give me a little credit for finding the hotel," Craig said.

"You're a brilliant man, Mr. Richmond."

"Don't you forget it, Mrs. Richmond." And then he winced. "I'm sorry. I didn't ask if you wanted to take my name, I just—"

"It's okay," she interrupted. "I like the sound of Tess Richmond. And it makes sense to have the same name my child will have."

He picked up the bottle of bubbly, studied the label. "I should call down to the desk to see if they have any nonalcoholic champagne."

"Don't worry about it," she said. "I don't need any champagne." The formalities of the wedding now over, she couldn't wait for Craig to take her in his arms again. Every nerve ending in her body hummed with the anticipation of being kissed until the world began to tilt.

He set down the bottle, then his eyes shifted and locked with hers. The intensity in his gaze stole the air from her lungs, made her head spin.

This is it, she thought. Now he would kiss her again.

Instead, he took a step in retreat. "I forgot to confirm our brunch reservations at the dining room."

And then, before she had a chance to respond, he was gone.

Tess sat on the edge of the bed and closed her eyes against the tears of confusion and frustration.

Dammit, he was the one who'd wanted this marriage. She hadn't asked him for anything, but he'd convinced her that they should be together, that they could be the family their baby deserved. And before the ink was even dry on their marriage certificate, he'd hightailed it out the door.

She swiped impatiently at the tears that slipped quietly down her cheeks and stood up to unfasten the zipper at the back of her dress.

Of all the ways she'd imagined spending her wedding night, this was not one of them. He'd promised to be right back, but she knew there was no sense in waiting up. He wouldn't come back until he was sure she was asleep. She didn't know where he'd gone—to the bar? The beach? The airport? It didn't really matter where he was. What mattered was that he wasn't with her.

He'd married her so that their child would have a stable home with two parents who loved him and he'd got what he wanted. The parents loving one another didn't come into play in his scenario.

But Tess did love him. She couldn't make him believe it or understand it any more than she could stop loving him. She could only hope that, over time, he might learn to love her, too. But that wasn't likely to happen if he couldn't even stand to be in the same room with her on their wedding night.

She wanted to stuff her dress into the garbage but reason won out over frustration and she hung it carefully in the closet instead. Then she stripped off her undergarments and opened the top drawer of the dresser rummaging inside for her nightgown. She heard the crinkle of tissue and pulled out the package Laurie had given to her before she left.

She unwrapped the tissue, examined the delicate silk and lace garment more suited to seduction than sleeping. Obviously, her sister hadn't planned for Tess to be alone on her wedding night, either. She hesitated, then impulsively slipped the nightgown over her head, the soft fabric sliding over her body like a caress, cool against her heated skin.

She took her time brushing her teeth, sat for a while in bed reading a novel, hoping that Craig would return even while she knew he wouldn't. After a long while, she finally gave up waiting and tried to sleep.

Craig cursed himself as he walked alone on the beach. He had to be a complete idiot to be out here on his wedding night, on his own, while his bride was in their honeymoon cottage getting ready for bed.

For weeks he'd been trying to deny the attraction between himself and Tess, focusing his efforts on courting her and trying not to think about the night they'd made love. His proposal might have originally been motivated by a desire to give his baby a family, but now that they were married he found himself wanting more. And right now, what he wanted was Tess in his bed.

He glanced back at the light visible in the bedroom and wished he could be in there with her now, holding her, touching her, loving her. But he couldn't forget her hesitation when he'd told her he wanted a real marriage. She'd seemed not only surprised but reluctant and it was that reluctance that gave him pause. Because no matter how much his body ached for the woman who was now his wife, she was still his friend and he didn't want to risk causing further damage to their relationship by pushing the boundaries she'd established.

She'd agreed to marry him so that their baby could have a full-time father, which was exactly what he'd wanted. Their marriage was a means to an end, a necessary step to guarantee his involvement in his child's life. He'd gotten exactly what he wanted.

So why did he feel so dissatisfied? Why did Tess's acquiescence suddenly bother him so much?

He picked up a round stone and tossed it toward the ocean. The pebble disappeared into the darkness, then plopped softly into the water.

He wanted to marry her, now he was married to her. So, why wasn't he happy?

Because he wanted *more*.

He wanted it all.

He almost laughed out loud at the ridiculously vague notion, made even more ridiculous by the realization that he already had it all. He had a challenging and rewarding career, a beautiful home in the suburbs, a child on the way. What else was there?

Love.

He ignored the soft taunt from his subconscious as he hurled another stone into the water.

He didn't believe in love or want any part of it. Love was a fickle and transient emotion, a weapon yielded to hurt and manipulate. No, he wasn't looking for love.

He wasn't looking for anything more than what he'd got by marrying Tess—a partnership with the mother of his child in a relationship unclouded by messy emotions.

Had Tess not heard the click of the door as it latched, she would still have known the exact moment Craig returned to the cottage. Over the past twenty-four hours, she'd become achingly aware of his presence and of his absence. She kept her eyes closed, waiting, wondering.

If he believed her to be asleep, would he crawl into bed beside her? If he did, she could just happen to roll over, to snuggle close against him.

She held her breath, hoped he couldn't hear the thunderous pounding of her heart over the hum of the air-conditioning unit. She sensed his hesitation, then let out a slow, frustrated breath as she heard his footsteps on the tile floor and the slide of the patio doors as he exited onto the deck.

Why did she care, anyway? Why was she so obsessed with a man who obviously didn't want to be with her?

Because he was her husband, dammit, and she loved him.

She opened her eyes, stared unseeing at the ceiling in the darkness.

Craig was the one who'd wanted this marriage. He'd all but forced her to walk down the aisle and now that his ring was firmly on her finger he thought he could ignore her. Tess felt the slow surge of anger. She was not going to let him ignore her.

She sat up in bed and swung her feet onto the floor. Striding purposefully across the room, she hesitated only briefly before sliding open the patio door and stepping out onto the deck.

Craig was seated on one of the padded chairs, his feet propped onto a stool. His eyes were closed, but she sensed the tension in his body.

"Craig?"

His eyes flew open and his head turned. "I thought you were asleep."

"I was waiting for you," she said softly.

She moved forward into the moonlight, heard his sharp intake of breath and fought back a smile. It sounded like Craig was impressed with the silk-and-lace peignoir that Laurie had given to her.

"Why?" he asked, his voice sounding a little strained.

She perched on the edge of the stool. One of the straps slid off her shoulder as she leaned forward, exposing the top curve of her breast. "I wanted to make sure you confirmed our reservations."

His gaze dipped to her cleavage. "Oh—yes."

She nodded. "Good."

"You should…uh…get some sleep."

"I'm not very tired."

"Oh. Okay."

He was flustered. It took a minute for the realization to sink in, but when it did, it helped ease some of the tension she was feeling.

Tess stretched her legs out in front of her, allowed her knee to brush against his as she extended it and he practically leapt out of his chair. He crossed to the edge of the deck, clamped his hands down on the railing.

She sighed. "You promised me this wouldn't happen."

"What are you talking about?"

"You said if we got married, I wouldn't ever lose you," she reminded him. "But ever since the night we slept together, there's been a distance between us that I don't know how to bridge and it just seems to be growing wider. Now I've got your ring on my finger, but you seem farther away from me than ever before." She felt her throat tighten and looked away so he wouldn't see the tears that blurred her eyes. "And I don't know what to do or how to fix us."

He moved back to where she was sitting, then held out his hand and drew her to her feet. "Things have changed," he agreed. "But I don't think there's anything that needs to be done or anything wrong that needs to be fixed."

"You can't tell me you're happy with the way things are between us right now."

His smile was wry. "No," he admitted.

"Then tell me what you want."

"You."

Her heart stuttered.

"If you want the truth—there it is," he told her. "It's not easy going back to being just friends after what happened. I can't be in the same room with you without thinking about that night. Without wanting you. It's a constant battle to keep my hands off of you."

Her earlier anger and frustration were forgotten as she tipped her head back to look at him. "I haven't asked you to keep your hands off of me."

"No, but I know your body's going through a lot of changes and—"

"And I want your hands on me."

"Oh, God, Tess."

She felt his grasp tighten on her fingers. "The day I agreed to marry you, you said that you wanted a real marriage," she reminded him. "Well, that's what I want, too. And I want it to start tonight."

His fingers were still laced with hers but he made no move toward her, and Tess knew he was making sure this was her decision. Her knees were trembling so badly she wondered that she was able to stand but she managed to raise herself onto her toes and touch her lips to his.

His body remained stiff, immobile but his lips molded to hers as he kissed her back. The nerves in her stomach dissolved, replaced by something stronger, fiercer, undeniable. She slid her hands up his chest, clasped them behind his head as she pressed her body against his. She heard him groan deep in his throat before he grasped her wrists in his hands and pulled away from her. He held her at arm's length, his breathing labored, his eyes dark with desire.

"Are you sure?" he asked hoarsely.

Tess smiled, no longer plagued by any doubts. "I want to make love with my husband." She wanted to show him, in actions if not in words, how much she loved him.

He released her hands and very gently cupped her face in his palms. He stroked his thumbs over her cheeks, the simple gesture surprisingly sensual. Then he slid his hands into her hair, tipping her head back so he could settle his lips over hers. His kiss was so soft, so tender, she felt as though her heart would melt.

She lost herself in his kiss, her earlier tears of disappointment and frustration forgotten. This was what she wanted, what she needed. She opened up her heart and her soul and she gave him everything that she had. Everything that she was.

He kissed her cheeks, her eyelids. "God, Tess, I want you so badly. But I didn't want to rush you."

At any other time, she might have taken exception to the fact that he'd been making decisions for her. Right now, however, she didn't care about anything but the passion that flared between them like a three-alarm blaze.

"Stop talking and kiss me again."

He did, covering her mouth at the same time that he lifted her around the waist and carried her back inside. He set her back on her feet beside the bed, but continued to ravish her mouth with hot, hungry kisses. His hands skimmed over her hips down to the hem of the silky nightgown, then beneath it. She heard her own sigh of satisfaction as his hands met the bare skin of her thighs. It seemed like an eternity since she'd felt his hands on her, since she'd had her hands on him.

She reached for the buttons of his shirt, fumbling in

her haste. His fingers circled her wrists, pulled her hands back down to her sides.

"I'm trying to take my time here," he whispered against her lips. "I want to enjoy touching you for a while."

"I want to touch you, too."

"Later," he promised, and released her hands to tug her nightgown over her head. He eased her back onto the bed and lowered himself beside her.

His hands moved to her breasts and she gasped as he brushed his thumbs over the already taut nipples, the contact sending ripples of pleasure through her body.

"They're heavier," he noted. "And fuller."

She nodded, surprised that he was aware of the subtle changes to her body.

"Are they more sensitive?" he asked, lowering his head to flick his tongue over one distended nipple.

She gasped again, arched instinctively toward him.

He raised his head to look at her and grinned. "I take it that's a yes?"

"Yes," she agreed breathlessly.

His tongue swirled around the peak, then his lips closed over it and Tess felt the heat begin to build inside her. He taunted her breast with his tongue, his teeth, until she was panting.

"I think the next few months are going to be a lot of fun." He lifted his head only long enough to murmur those words, then turned his attention to her other breast.

Tess moaned and writhed beneath him.

"Oh, yeah, this is going to be fun."

She grasped his shoulders, digging her nails into the firm muscles as she tried to maintain some equilibrium as the world spun around her. She'd never felt so close to losing complete control just by having her breasts massaged. Then again, she'd never felt anything before like she felt with Craig. Every touch, every kiss, left her breathless, eager for more.

"Craig...please..."

He skimmed his hands over her body, slowly, his fingertips barely making contact with her skin, yet she burned everywhere he touched and her breath quickened in response to the teasing caresses.

Desperate to feel the warmth of his skin under her hands, she tugged at the front of his shirt, mindless of the buttons that flew as she tore it open.

Craig chuckled against her mouth. "That was a good shirt."

"It was in the way." She pushed the shirt off his shoulders, ran her hands down the smooth planes of his chest. She found the buckle of his belt, worked it free. He kissed her hard on the mouth, then rolled away from her and off the bed to shed the rest of his clothes. She hadn't realized she'd been holding her breath until he lay down again beside her, his flesh bare and hot against hers, and she was able to breathe again.

The hard muscles of his chest brushed the tips of her nipples and caused twin arrows of heat to spread from the point of contact to the throbbing warmth between her thighs. She thrust her hips toward him, wordlessly seeking the fulfillment only he could give her. But he held back, teasing her with featherlight caresses, soft kisses.

"Not yet," he whispered the words against her lips. "I've only just begun."

And he continued his exquisite torture, relentlessly

driving her higher and higher. She was quivering beneath him, her body strung tight as a bow. Sensation upon sensation seemed to assault her from every direction as he continued to stroke her body with his hands, his lips, his tongue. Desire such as she'd never experienced slammed into her with the force of a freight train.

She fisted her hands in the sheet as his hand skimmed over the curve of her belly and found the tangle of curls between her thighs. He slid a finger inside the slick, wet heat. She shuddered and screamed out his name as the intimate intrusion pushed her over the edge.

Then he raised himself over her, pressing her into the mattress with his body. She welcomed his weight, parted her thighs to urge him closer.

"I've never wanted anyone the way I want you, Tess."

He buried himself inside her in one sure stroke. Tess gasped and clutched his shoulders, her nails biting into his flesh. She'd forgotten how big he was, how completely he filled her, fulfilled her. He began to move inside her, slow, steady strokes that seemed to touch her very soul. As she lifted her hips in response to the rhythm he'd set, she felt herself climbing again, soaring.

This time, when the spasms rocked her body, he went with her.

Chapter Ten

"**I**'m crushing you," Craig said, murmuring the words into her hair. He knew he should roll off of her, but right now he couldn't even move. It was a wonder he could even speak, his climax had so completely drained him.

Was it the anticipation, he wondered, that had made their lovemaking so phenomenal?

Or was it Tess?

"I'm okay," she told him, her fingertips tracing lazily down his back. "Better than okay."

He managed to lift his head enough to look at her. "Better than okay?"

Her eyes were closed, but her lips curved. "Much better."

"How much better?"

Her lashes fluttered, revealing beautiful blue eyes

still dark with passion. "Do you want a number on a scale of one to ten?"

"Of course not."

Her eyes drifted shut again.

"Maybe."

She chuckled softly. "Twelve."

He was grateful her eyes were closed, so she couldn't see him grinning like an idiot. He was relieved to know that the most incredible, mind-numbing sexual experience of his life hadn't been a disappointment for Tess.

Twelve, she'd said.

Well, weeks of wanting her, dreaming about her, had eroded his self-control. He was willing to bet he could do better next time.

He tipped his head to kiss her, skimmed a hand over her breast. She murmured and wriggled beneath him, the movement eliciting an immediate response from his own body. He deepened the kiss.

Oh, yeah, he'd do much better this time.

When Tess awoke the following morning, she didn't have the usual impulse to get up and get moving. No, she felt far too content this morning to want to be anywhere other than exactly where she was: snuggled under the sheets in Craig's arms. Craig Richmond—her oldest and dearest friend and now her husband.

If she allowed herself to think about it, she might still worry that marrying Craig was an impulse she'd eventually regret. But it was hard to believe that when her skin still tingled from his touch, when her body was molded to the warmth of his own. Sometime over the past few weeks she'd managed to convince herself that the out-of-control passion she'd experienced that first night had been an anomaly. Or that the memories had been distorted by her imagination and her newly-discovered feelings for him. But last night had proven her wrong.

They'd barely spoken to one another throughout their lovemaking marathon, communicating their wants and needs with their bodies rather than words. Every stroke of his fingertips, every touch of her lips, every brush of their flesh, carried a message of want, of need. Time and time again, passion had flared between them, burning higher and brighter and stronger until it consumed them both. And then they'd finally slept, their heads side by side on one pillow, their limbs still entwined.

With Craig, she really felt as though she were making love and not just having sex. The depth of his passion overwhelmed her; the power of her response stunned her. She had never experienced anything like it with anyone else and she knew she never would. Because she knew now that the reason she responded to Craig so completely, the reason he'd been able to touch a part inside her that no one else had ever come close to finding, was because she loved him.

And she was scared. How much longer could she keep up the charade of their marriage without revealing her feelings for him? She'd always thought that sex and love were separate entities, but now she knew differently. Making love with Craig was more than the physical union of two bodies, it was an experience that touched the very center of her soul. She was so afraid he would realize that when she shared her body, she was sharing her heart. And yet, she could no more withhold herself than she could withhold her love.

"I can almost hear you thinking." His words, murmured so close to her ear, startled her.

"I thought you were sleeping."

"I was, but I'm awake now." He skimmed a hand down her side, over the slope of her hip, down her thigh.

She leaned her head back against his chest, savored being in the warmth of his embrace. But she knew that although she'd fallen head over heels for Craig, he'd only married her because of the baby. She wanted their marriage to work, but more than anything she wanted him to be happy.

He turned her in his arms, brushed a light kiss against her lips.

Tess pulled back. "If at any time you change your mind, if you decide this isn't what you want, will you tell me?"

He smoothed the line above her brow with his finger. "Haven't we already had this discussion?"

"Just promise me that you'll let me know if you don't want to stay married."

"I've had lots of time to think about this—too much time. I'm not going to change my mind." He kissed her again, lingered. "When we exchanged those vows, I meant every word. I've made a promise to you, Tess. To you and our baby. And I will be there for you, forever."

She wanted to believe him. But in those vows he'd also promised to love her and although she knew Craig cared about her, he wasn't in love with her. And that was the only thing that was missing. If Craig loved her, if this was a real marriage—based on shared hopes and dreams instead of an inopportune pregnancy—she'd be the happiest woman alive.

Still, she was happy. And relieved. She knew that

Craig would stand by her and that he'd be a father to their baby. It would have to be enough. She had no right to ask for, or expect, anything more.

"And I'm not going to let you change your mind, either," Craig said. "I will do everything I can to make our marriage work, to make you happy."

"I am happy," she told him.

"Good." He sat up abruptly. "By the way, I have something for you."

"What?"

"A wedding gift." He threw off the covers and swung his legs over the side of the bed. Unconcerned about his nakedness, he crossed the room and pulled something out of the front pocket of his suitcase.

"You already gave me the best gift," she told him, "bringing my sister and her family here for the wedding."

"Then I'm hoping this will be a second-best gift." He climbed back onto the bed and handed her a large envelope.

She turned it over and tore open the flap, her brow creased in concentration as she examined the official-looking document.

It was a property deed, transferring one-half ownership of the house he'd bought to her. Tess stared at the paper for the longest time, not certain what she should do or say. No one had ever given her a house—or anything remotely like it—before.

"I don't know what to say," she admitted at last. "I never expected… I mean…it's *your* house."

"It's *our* house now," he said.

"But you bought it. I can't—"

"Yes, you can. I bought it for us—for our family."

"But…"

He tugged the deed out of her hand and tossed it aside. "It's done, forget about it."

She scowled. "Will you let me say one thing?"

He hesitated. "All right."

"Thank you." She was still uncomfortable with the enormity of the gesture, but she understood that sharing his home was Craig's way of showing that he wanted her and the baby with him and she couldn't reject such generosity.

"You're welcome."

"I didn't get you anything," Tess said. Everything had happened so fast, she'd never even had a chance to think about a wedding gift for Craig.

"You've given me far more than you realize." He splayed his palm over the gentle curve of her belly. "Although it's still hard to believe there's a baby growing inside you."

She put her hand over his. "He's still really tiny."

"How tiny?"

"About two-and-a-half inches."

"Wow." He rubbed his hand in gentle circles. "Does he look like a baby?"

"I don't know. I'll get to see him when I have the ultrasound in a couple more months."

"Why are you having an ultrasound? Is everything all right? Are you feeling okay?"

The immediate concern in his voice made her smile. "I'm fine, the baby's fine. It's a routine procedure, just to check on the baby's development."

"Oh." He exhaled audibly. Then asked, "Can I come with you?"

Tess smiled. "If you'd like."

"Yeah, I would. I want to be there with you, every step of the way."

And he would, she knew, because that was the type of man he was. He would be there for her and he would love their child. He just wouldn't love her.

Craig kissed her lightly. "What has you looking so sad all of a sudden?"

She forced another smile. "I'm not sad, I was just thinking."

"About what?"

"How very lucky our baby is going to be."

The six days they spent on the island after their wedding were so idyllic that Tess hadn't wanted to leave. They'd taken various tours around the island—a cigar factory, a rum distillery, an historic plantation house. They'd enjoyed a five-hour catamaran cruise that included snorkeling and swimming with turtles. They'd walked into Bridgetown and picked up some touristy souvenirs. It had truly been a magical trip and she couldn't remember any time in her life when she'd ever been happier.

The plane touched down on the runway and she felt a pang of regret that the honeymoon was now officially over. It was now time to get back to reality, to face the world and the inevitable questions and speculation about their hasty marriage—not that people would be speculating for too long before her pregnancy became obvious—and remember that Craig had only married her to give their baby a family.

The thought shouldn't have hurt as much as it did.

After all, Craig never made any promises of love. Nor had she for that matter. At least, not out loud. They'd both been concentrating on practical considerations when they'd decided to marry.

But when she'd promised to love, honor and cherish him, she'd meant every single word. She would never have been able to recite those vows otherwise. And they'd been so close over the past few days, she'd started to hope that his feelings for her might be growing as well. But maybe it was nothing more than the newly-discovered passion between them—and how long could she expect that to last when her pregnancy started to show?

She listened to the announcement on the speaker asking all passengers to remain seated with their belts fastened.

"What are you thinking about?" Craig asked.

"That a week has never gone by so quickly."

"I know what you mean." He brushed a strand of hair away from her face, stroked a finger along the edge of her jaw. "We had a good time, didn't we?"

She nodded.

"You know," he said, "this plane refuels and goes back."

She had to admit there was a part of her that wished they could have stayed in their enchanting paradise a little longer. Maybe even forever. But as tempting as the idea was, it was unrealistic. "We had to come back sometime."

There was a ding as the seat-belt light went out and people began to scramble out of their seats, digging through overhead bins for their carry-on luggage. Tess unbuckled her belt.

"You're worried, aren't you?" Craig asked.

She wasn't surprised that he sensed the reason for her melancholy. "Everything will be different here. People are bound to talk about the hastiness of our marriage and it won't be long before they know why we got married."

"And that bothers you?"

"Of course, it does. I don't want anyone thinking that I tricked you into this marriage, that I'm taking advantage of you."

"No one who knows me would believe that," Craig said dryly, reaching into the overhead compartment for their bags.

"Maybe," Tess acknowledged. But she knew there would be plenty who thought so just the same.

When they got home from the airport, Craig carried their bags into the house after giving firm instructions to Tess to wait outside.

He came back a few minutes later, swept her into his arms and carried her over the threshold. He set her back on her feet in the foyer and placed a soft kiss on her lips.

"Welcome home, Tess."

And with those words, her tension eased.

She followed him upstairs, carrying only her shoulder bag as Craig insisted the luggage was heavy. Too weary to argue, she let the comment pass. His protective attitude would likely get worse as her pregnancy progressed and she decided that she'd better learn to pick her battles. And really, she didn't mind letting a man carry her suitcase.

She paused in the doorway of the master bedroom. She'd been in here before, when he'd first brought her to see the house but the room had been freshly painted since then and his furniture moved in.

"What are you smirking about?" Craig asked, setting their suitcases down on the far side of the room.

"I'd been thinking that I was sorry our honeymoon was over," she admitted. "And then I got a look at your bed."

He raised his eyebrows.

"It's as big as the one we had in Barbados."

"All the better to ravish you in," he said, sweeping her into his arms and rolling with her on top of the plaid comforter.

She giggled as he nuzzled her neck, biting playfully on her nape. "And do you intend to ravish me?" she asked breathlessly.

His hands were already working the buttons on her blouse. "Oh, yeah."

She sighed as his hands skimmed over her bare skin. She knew she could always rely on Craig to keep his promises.

Craig was indulging in a second cup of coffee and scanning the newspaper as he waited for Tess to finish in the bathroom. He'd been tempted to join her in the shower, but the couple of times they'd tried that the cleansing ritual had rapidly turned into foreplay. Not that he had any complaints, but Tess had firmly banned him from the bathroom this morning so they wouldn't be late for Becca's birthday party.

Three weeks had passed since they'd been pro-nounced husband and wife and he found that he'd adapted easily to this marriage thing. In fact, he was quite enjoying being married to Tess, waking up with her every morning, spending hours making love with her. She was the most incredibly passionate woman he'd ever known and the woman he really believed he could be happy with for the rest of his life.

For the baby's sake, of course.

Because that was what their marriage was about—giving their child a family. The fact that he and Tess were so obviously compatible was a nice bonus but he wasn't going to complicate their relationship by imagining that his feelings for Tess were growing. No, it was sex, it was simple. And he intended to keep it that way.

He heard the shower shut off and contemplated going upstairs to help Tess towel off. But as he set the newspaper aside to do just that, the phone rang. He was hanging up when Tess walked into the room, fully dressed, a few minutes later.

"What is that in your shampoo?" he asked, sniffing her hair as she moved past him to turn on the kettle.

"What do you mean?"

"The scent," he said impatiently. "What is it?"

She found a cup and plopped a tea bag into it. "Apples, I think. Why?"

He'd thought that's what it was—he'd just never expected to find the fragrance of fruit so arousing. "It's sexy."

"Sexy?" She glanced up, her eyebrows raised in disbelief. "My shampoo?"

"You have no idea how many nights I used to lie awake, unable to get the scent of your shampoo out of my mind."

"Really?" She was clearly intrigued by this revelation.

"Really." He stepped behind her, inhaling deeply as he dipped his head to nuzzle her throat. It was, he'd quickly learned, one of her most erogenous zones and the quick shiver that ran through her body proved it.

"Craig," she said warningly.

"Hmm?" He slid his arms around her, tucking her back against his front.

"We have to go shopping this morning to get a birthday present for my niece."

"I know." He reluctantly stepped away as Tess reached for the now boiling kettle.

"And then we have dinner at your parents' house later."

"Yeah—Mom just called to remind me."

"Are we going to tell them about the baby tonight?"

"We probably shouldn't wait too much longer," he said. "But I don't know if tonight is too soon. My dad was shocked enough by the news we were getting married—finding out he's going to be a grandfather so soon might give him heart failure."

She sipped at the herbal tea he'd been encouraging her to drink instead of coffee, made a face.

She claimed it tasted like flowers but she tolerated it anyway. At least when he was around. She still snuck coffee when she didn't think he was looking, so, unbeknownst to her, he'd replaced his regular grind with decaf. He missed the caffeine jolt himself but figured it was a small sacrifice to make for the health of their baby.

"Craig?"

"Hmm…" he said, unable to remember what they'd been talking about.

Tess shook her head. "I think the lack of caffeine is hindering your brain function."

He frowned and stared into his cup. "How did you know about the coffee?"

"It tastes like decaf," she told him. "As for sharing the news of my pregnancy, I don't think we'll be able to wait too much longer—not at the rate this baby seems to be growing."

He sipped his coffee, secretly acknowledging that she was right about the taste. "Yes, well, I think there's something I should tell you in that regard."

"About the baby, or the coffee?"

"The baby," he clarified.

She looked at him suspiciously. "What?"

He refilled his mug. "Big babies seem to run in my family."

"Big?" Tess echoed. "How big?" She took another sip of her tea.

"My brother was a little over nine pounds." He shot her a look of apology. "I was almost ten."

She choked, coughed. "Ten pounds? Why didn't you tell me this before?"

"It's not as if we could do anything about it," he pointed out reasonably.

"But *ten* pounds?" She was clearly stunned. "Well, it would explain why none of my clothes are fitting anymore."

"It might also explain why my mother left," he joked.

She didn't laugh.

"It's hard not to think about her, isn't it?" she asked gently. "Now that you're going to have a child of your own."

He didn't like to admit it, but he knew he couldn't hide the truth from her. "It scares me sometimes, to think that I could walk out on my child like she did."

"You couldn't," she assured him. "You wouldn't

have fought so hard to be part of your baby's life if you had any doubts."

"But there was a time—at least I think there was—when she wanted me and Gage, too."

Tess pushed away from the table to stand behind his chair, wrapped her arms around his shoulders. "She made the biggest mistake of her life when she walked out on you," she said. "You're smarter than that."

"Do you really think so?"

"Yes, I do."

He turned his head to look at her. "Do you know what I think?"

"What?"

He pulled her onto his lap. "I think that marrying you was the smartest thing I ever did."

Tess stayed late at the office on Friday, surfing the Net for job postings. There were plenty of employers looking for software programmers, just none in the immediate vicinity of Pinehurst or even within a reasonable commuting distance. But there were some IT support positions available so she printed copies of those that sounded interesting.

She hadn't had a chance to update her résumé yet, unwilling to use the computer at home because she hadn't yet told Craig about the fate of SBG. She was going to, of course, but she wanted to have another job lined up first. She didn't want him to feel compelled to find something for her at Richmond.

She wouldn't trade on their relationship for a job when she was a recent college graduate looking for work and she especially wouldn't do so now that they were husband

and wife. But with only a few weeks left until the transition took place she was quickly running out of time.

And running behind schedule she noticed when she glanced at the clock.

She grabbed the pages from the printer and tucked them into her purse on her way out of the office. A week, she promised herself. If she hadn't resolved her job situation in a week she'd tell him anyway rather than run the risk of him finding out from someone else.

She made a quick stop on the way home to pick up Chinese food because it was her night to cook and she hadn't taken anything out of the freezer for dinner. Of course, Craig would tease her that she'd purposely forgotten—and maybe she had. But she'd had other things on her mind before she'd left for work that morning. Most notably the fact that, after a three-day conference in Boston, her husband was finally going to be home tonight.

She was just unpacking dinner when he got in. He dropped his briefcase on the floor and pulled her into his arms.

"Isn't a dutiful wife supposed to be waiting at the door when her husband gets home?" he teased when he finally ended the kiss so they could both catch their breath.

"I'm kind of new at this wife thing," she reminded him.

"Did you miss me?" he asked, his hands moving down the front of her sweater, deftly unfastening buttons along the way.

"Stop that," she protested, swatting at his hands in order to avoid answering his question. Because she'd missed him more than she wanted to admit. "I'm trying to be a good wife by getting your dinner on the table."

"I've been waiting—" he glanced at his watch "—sixty-three hours to get my hands on you."

She couldn't help but smile, because sixty-three hours was exactly right by her calculations, too. "I thought you'd be hungry," she told him.

"I am," he assured her, and kissed her again.

She sighed into his mouth, her tongue meeting and mating with his.

His hands slid down her back, over the curve of her buttocks, pulling her tight against him. She was suddenly conscious of the slight bulge of her tummy and worried that her growing belly would diminish his ardor. But there was no hint of disinterest in the way he was touching her and her concerns melted away in the heat of their passion.

She reached between their bodies to tug at the button of his pants, push the zipper down. Then she slid her hand inside his boxers and wrapped her fingers around the solid length of him. A groan rumbled deep in his throat as he pushed up her skirt and quickly discarded her panties.

He lifted her off her feet, bracing her against the granite countertop. It was cold and hard, but she didn't care. She was focused on the heat of his skin and the glorious strength of his body as she wrapped her legs around his hips. She cried out as he plunged into her and her head fell back, her fingers gripping his shoulders, as the first waves of pleasure swamped her.

She'd never known such unbridled passion—hadn't thought she was capable of acting so outrageously. They hadn't even bothered to remove their clothes—other than what was absolutely necessary to enable them to complete the act. It was all so primitive, almost violent. And so incredibly erotic.

He dipped his head, his teeth scraping over the lace-covered peak of her breast, and she gasped. Then his lips closed around the aching nub, suckling wetly through the fabric, until she felt her core shatter into a billion kaleidoscopic pieces.

And still he continued the delicious torment—his mouth, his hands and his deep steady thrusts driving her again and again to the edge—and beyond.

Relentlessly, mindlessly, gloriously beyond.

She didn't know how long they stayed there, bodies locked together, braced against the counter. She vaguely wondered if she should be shocked by what had just happened, but she was too satisfied to feel anything but blissfully content.

"God, Tess, no one has ever made me lose control like you do." He sounded bewildered, almost angry, but his hands were gentle as he eased her feet back to the ground.

"Should I apologize?" she asked, when she was finally able to speak.

He smiled, somewhat ruefully. "No. It's just that…" He stepped away to fasten his pants, shook his head. "This wasn't what I wanted."

She frowned as she buttoned her sweater. "I thought it was what we both wanted."

"I was thinking about making love with you the whole way home," he admitted. "But I didn't expect it to happen like this. I should have been able to control my desire, to be careful with you—to at least wait until we were in the bedroom."

He shook his head again. "I missed you so much, Tess. I was only gone three days and I missed you."

A tiny spark of hope flickered in Tess's heart. Was it possible, she wondered, that Craig was starting to have feelings for her? That she was more to him than the mother of his child?

She cupped his face in her hands, kissed him gently. "I missed you, too."

"Yeah?" He seemed pleased by the thought.

"Yeah."

"I don't understand what's happening," he said, sounding bewildered again. "This was supposed to be simple. We got married to give our baby a family, to give him a secure and stable home. This—" he gestured vaguely. "You—me. I don't understand why it seems so complicated all of a sudden."

The tiny spark flared a little brighter.

"I thought it was just that I've gotten used to having you around, but it's more than that. Dammit, Tess, I need you." He turned away from her, scrubbed his hands through his hair. His next words were barely a whisper. "I've never needed anyone before."

She hated the anguish she heard in his voice, hated that he was fighting so hard against the feelings he had for her and secretly thrilled to realize that he *did* have feelings for her.

Maybe the fairy tale wasn't so far beyond her reach, after all.

Chapter Eleven

The food at Marco's was always fabulous, the portions generous and the service prompt. Tess pushed aside her plate and sighed in contentment at the end of another sinfully indulgent meal.

"Okay, now you can tell me the truth," Craig said. "Were you really craving spinach-and-ricotta ravioli or did you just want to get out of cooking tonight?"

"Does it matter?" she asked. "I'm sure you enjoyed your chicken marsala more than you would have meat loaf."

"I can't disagree with that, although you do make a great meat loaf."

"I make a passable meatloaf," she corrected. "We both know I'm not very creative in the kitchen."

"As I remember, you were very creative in the kitchen Friday night."

Tess hoped the candlelight concealed her flaming cheeks. "I was referring to cooking."

He smiled. "Are you blushing, Tess?"

Obviously the light wasn't dim enough. "No, I'm not blushing." She felt her cheeks burn even hotter. She was twenty-nine years old, it was ridiculous to be blushing. "It's warm in here."

He continued to smile, clearly not accepting her explanation for a moment.

"Did you remember that I have a doctor's appointment tomorrow?" she asked in a blatant attempt to change the subject.

He nodded. "It's on my calendar at work."

"Were you planning to come?"

"Definitely," he said. "We should be able to hear our baby's heartbeat this time."

She'd thought his interest in her pregnancy might wane after a few weeks but he was constantly surprising her with information or questions about the baby growing inside her.

"Have you been reading pregnancy books again?" she asked.

"Internet research," he corrected.

"Have you been researching baby names, too?"

He'd started tossing out name suggestions a couple of days earlier, mostly outrageous and ridiculous suggestions that she didn't take seriously except as a reminder that they did need to choose some possible names for their baby.

"I've come up with a few more names," he admitted.

"Such as?"

"Esmeralda."

Tess made a face.

"Jasmine."

She shook her head.

"Ariel."

"Can you try to be serious about this?"

"I'm trying," he said. "But what if we pick a name, say Sarah, and she doesn't look anything like a Sarah?"

"What, exactly, does a Sarah look like?" she countered.

He scowled. "You know what I mean. You might think you have the perfect name picked out and then find it doesn't suit the baby once she's born."

"You're right," she agreed. "After all, Sarah would be as completely inappropriate as Esmeralda, Jasmine or Ariel for a boy."

"You really think it's going to be a boy?"

"I think we should pick out a boy's name and a girl's name," she said.

"In case we have twins?"

She glared at him across the table. "We are *not* having twins."

"You don't want more than one baby?" he asked.

"I want to have one at a time."

"Then we only need one name," he pointed out reasonably.

She was helpless to prevent the smile that curved her lips. He was so often difficult, occasionally infuriating and somehow always irresistibly charming.

Her smile froze when she recognized the woman approaching their table. It was Lana—Craig's former fiancée—and she looked absolutely stunning in a pink spandex dress that showed off her flawless figure.

Even before Tess got pregnant, she wouldn't have had the confidence to wear such a revealing outfit. Nor, she was forced to admit, would it have looked half as good on her. And now—well, she wasn't quite into maternity clothes yet, but she was wearing only the loosest-fitting pieces in her wardrobe. Tonight she had on a long tunic-style top over a wraparound skirt that mostly disguised the slight curve of her belly.

"Mr. and Mrs. Richmond," Lana greeted them in a falsely sweet tone. "How are the happy newlyweds?"

"We're fine, thanks." Craig's tone was clipped, cool—clearly signaling that he was less than pleased by the interruption.

Lana tossed her immaculate blond hair over her shoulder, unaffected by the lack of warmth in his response. "I almost didn't believe it when I heard the rumor you'd married," she went on, her gaze moving from Craig to Tess, then dropping pointedly to Tess's belly. "Then I heard that you were going to be a daddy—and suddenly it made sense."

"Lana…" There was an unmistakable note of warning in Craig's voice.

She laughed softly, derisively. "Come on, Craig. Are you really going to tell me that you didn't marry her because she was pregnant?" There was a nasty edge to the question, a malicious challenge in her tone.

"Why Tess and I got married is none of your business," he said tightly.

Tess had thought she was prepared for the snide remarks that would follow the disclosure of her pregnancy, but this encounter proved that she hadn't been prepared at all. Not for someone like Lana. And not for

Craig's response to undermine all of her hopes for their relationship.

She knew when they got married that he'd only wanted to secure his place in their child's life, but over the past several weeks she'd allowed herself to hope that things had changed. That he was starting to love her, too. Obviously she'd been wrong.

"But it is my business," Lana retorted. "After all, you put a ring on my finger once, too."

"You put the ring on your own finger," Craig said. "All I had to do was pay for it."

Lana's cheeks flushed, with embarrassment or anger, Tess wasn't sure, as she turned from her former fiancé to his new wife.

"I really do want to congratulate you," she said to Tess. "If I'd known that getting knocked up was the key to holding on to a man like Craig, I might have done it myself." Her gaze drifted downward again, then she shrugged. "I imagine it's a comfort to know you'll at least have your baby when he grows bored with you."

Then, with a satisfied smile, she turned and sauntered away.

Craig reached across the table to take her hand. "Please don't let her get to you," he said.

"You've dated a lot of women over the years. Something like this was bound to happen sooner or later." Tess strove to keep her tone light, to hide her hurt as she disentangled her hand from his. "And I can understand that she would be upset about your marriage when it wasn't so long ago that you were engaged to her."

"It was almost two years ago," he said. "And she's been married *and* divorced since then."

"But she obviously loved you at one time and you must have loved her."

"I'm not sure love had anything to do with it. Love was only a tool Lana used to get what she wanted."

Tess flinched at the bitterness in his tone. Whatever feelings he'd had for his ex, there was no denying how much she'd hurt him.

"That's no reason to give up on love," she said gently.

He just shook his head. "I'm sorry about Lana. She's obviously still angry with me and you just got caught in the crossfire."

She wanted to believe him, but she had to ask, "How long do you think it will be until you grow bored with me?"

"I won't," he promised. "You're it for me—my best friend, my wife and the mother of my child and that's all I need."

Tess let it go. She knew she had no right to ask for anything more.

Craig was doing something he rarely did—playing hooky from work. But he didn't feel too guilty about it because his boss was playing hooky, too. Actually, they were spending the afternoon playing golf because beating up on a dimpled white ball was one of his father's favorite ways of clearing the mind and the Pinehurst Golf Club was his venue of choice when he wanted to talk to either of his sons.

When Craig had agreed to this game, he'd wondered about the real purpose behind the invitation. But having played through sixteen holes without any business issues or family matters being dropped into the conversation, Craig began to suspect that maybe his dad had really just wanted to play golf.

Now they were on the green at the par-four seventeenth. Rather Allan was on the green, having driven his second shot from the fairway to drop about twelve feet from the flag. Craig had needed a third shot to chip his ball onto the green but was still only on the edge of it.

About thirty feet to the hole, he guessed, as he pulled his putter out of his bag. A difficult but not impossible shot.

His dad removed the flag and stepped out of the way.

Craig didn't worry too much about sinking his putt, he just wanted to move his ball closer to the hole so he was even more surprised than his father when the ball actually rolled straight into the cup.

"Nice shot," Allan said.

"Lucky shot," he corrected.

His dad shook his head as he crouched down to study the slope of the green. "You're on your game today."

"I'm still two strokes behind you."

Allan glanced up at him and grinned. "Usually it's about five."

Craig acknowledged the point with a nod as his father lined up his shot.

He tapped it gently. It rolled toward the hole, circled the lip then dropped in.

"Now I'm three back," Craig said, noting the scores on the card.

His dad retrieved the balls from the cup, tossed Craig's to him.

"I have to admit," Allan said, "I was a little concerned when you showed up at my office the day you told me you were getting married. But I have no doubts anymore that it was the right decision for you. You seem happier and more relaxed than I can ever remember you being."

Craig fell into step beside him as they crossed over the wooden bridge to the eighteenth tee. "I am happy," he admitted. "Tess fits into my life, so much that I already can't imagine being without her."

Allan smiled. "You know your mother's feeling pretty smug about this whole thing."

"Why's that?" Craig took his driver out of his bag and a tee out of his pocket.

"Because she told me more than ten years ago that you'd end up with Tess."

"You're kidding."

His father shook his head. "You'd just come home after your first year of college and you looked at her as if you were seeing her for the first time."

Craig remembered the moment—the realization that the tomboy friend he'd said goodbye to in September had somehow turned into an attractive woman in the eight months he'd been gone. It had been a surprise and a temptation.

But Tess had given no indication that her feelings had changed, so he'd kept his own under wraps and they'd fallen back into their usual routines. And that had been that—until the night he'd slept with her.

He pushed the memory of that night out of his mind to focus on the ball in front of him. He set his feet, drew back his club and connected.

"Nice." His dad watched the ball soar through the air

and drop into the middle of the fairway, leaving Craig in good position to birdie the hole. "And then you went and got engaged to Lana and Grace laid awake at night worried you were going to spend the rest of your life with the wrong woman."

"She never said anything about that to me."

"Of course not," Allan agreed. "You were thirty years old—old enough to make your own choices—and your own mistakes."

Craig remained silent while his father set up to tee off. He didn't want to talk about Lana, but he couldn't dismiss the comments she'd made at the restaurant only two days earlier.

He didn't believe she'd heard about Tess's pregnancy—more likely she'd only been speculating as to the reason for his marriage because of the quickness of it. But he hadn't been able to deny it, not when Tess was starting to show and the pregnancy would be readily obvious to everyone in a couple of months and he knew he needed to tell his parents before they heard it from someone else.

He heard the whoosh of air, the thunk of the club face against the ball, then watched the white sphere rise high and higher against the blue sky before dropping on the fairway—about ten yards behind Craig's ball. Ordinarily that would be enough for him to make some teasing comment about his father's game slipping but there was something else on his mind.

"Dad…"

"Hmm?" Alan dropped his club into his bag and started walking up the fairway.

Craig fell into step beside him again trying to find the

right words to tell his father about the baby. In the end, he figured straightforward was best. "Tess is pregnant."

His dad surprised him by nodding. "I sort of figured that when you were in such a hurry to get married."

"I should have told you then," Craig admitted. "But I knew you'd be disappointed."

"Actually, I'm kind of intrigued by the idea of being a grandfather. And your mother is over the moon."

"I think I knew you'd be pleased about that but I was worried that you'd be disappointed in me."

"Why?" Allan pulled his seven-iron out of his bag and set up beside his ball.

"Because we had the talk about safe sex and contraception."

"Sometimes all the precautions in the world can't overcome the whims of fate." His second shot landed just short of the green.

"I just wanted you to know that I wasn't careless," Craig told him. "I wouldn't be—especially not with Tess."

"I don't need the details," his dad told him.

Craig managed a smile as he carried his eight iron over to his ball. "I wasn't going to share them."

"Good." Allan was silent while Craig took his shot, nodding when it landed on the green.

Then he surprised the hell out of his son by saying, "Grace was pregnant when we got married. We were planning to get married, anyway, but we moved up the schedule when we found out she was expecting. She lost the baby a few weeks later."

Craig grabbed his bag and scrambled after his father. When he caught up and found his voice all he could think to say was, "I had no idea."

Allan shrugged. "You and Gage were both kids—it wasn't the kind of information we would have shared with you then."

"I always wondered why you never had any more kids."

"We wanted to and we kept trying for a while. But Grace had three more miscarriages during the first five years of our marriage. And I finally had a vasectomy," his dad admitted, "because I couldn't bear to go through it all over again—the excitement, the hope, the devastation. I always worried that it was harder for Grace because she had no children of her own. She would have been a great mother."

"She *is* a great mother," Craig said.

His father smiled. "You're right. She is."

They played out the hole—this time Craig earned the birdie, Allan the par, which meant that father still finished two strokes ahead of son.

"That means you're buying the beer," Allan reminded him as they made their way toward the clubhouse.

"Good thing it's a payday," Craig joked. Then, more seriously, "I never thought about the possibility that Tess could lose this baby. I don't know what we'd do if she did."

"I didn't tell you about the miscarriages to make you worry. I only wanted you to realize that things don't always work out the way we plan. And as difficult as it was for both of us to deal with each loss we always knew we had each other. When you hit the rough spots in your marriage—and believe me, no matter how rosy everything seems right now, there will be rough spots— just remember that you love her."

Craig didn't correct his father's assumption, he

didn't tell him that the subject of marriage would never have come up except that Tess got pregnant. Because he believed that the reasons for their marriage didn't matter so long as they were both committed to making it work and didn't try to complicate their relationship with unwanted emotions.

He tucked his sunglasses into his pocket as he followed his father into the clubhouse. They'd just been seated and ordered their drinks when his dad raised his arm, waving to someone across the room.

Craig glanced over his shoulder to see one of Tess's bosses, Owen Sanderson, and his wife, Peggy, making their way toward them.

"Why don't you join us?" Allan invited. "Craig's buying today."

"Old man beat you again, huh?" Peggy teased, as Owen pulled back one of the vacant chairs at their table for her.

"He always does," Craig agreed easily.

"Well, today drinks are on us," Owen insisted. "To celebrate your recent marriage and my impending retirement."

Tess was already home when Craig got back after the round of golf with his father, standing in front of the stove cooking dinner.

It was a picture most men would envy: a beautiful woman—his wife—greeting him with a smile and a ready meal at the end of the day. He knew that he could go to her, put his arms around her and she would tip her head back to meet his lips with her own. Then they would turn off the stove and go upstairs and on the way, he'd be thanking his lucky stars that he'd managed to convince this incredible woman to marry him.

Even now, knowing what he did, he couldn't stop himself from wanting her. And so he stayed where he was in the doorway to the kitchen.

She smiled when she saw him standing there. "Laurie put together a binder of simple recipes she promised that even I couldn't screw up, so I thought I'd try cooking something other than meat loaf tonight."

Putting a lid over the pan she started toward him, the easy smile still on her face. "How was your game?"

It would be easy to fall into the routine, to pretend nothing had changed. But he couldn't ignore the sense of betrayal that ate away inside him. He couldn't believe that the woman he trusted more than any other had lied to him.

"When did you know that SB Graphics was selling out to GigaPix?" he asked.

Her steps faltered, her smile faded. "How did you find out?"

"I ran into Owen Sanderson and his wife at the golf course."

She winced, confirming the guilt he'd wanted her to be able to deny.

"They'd just booked an Alaskan cruise to celebrate his retirement."

"Peggy suffered a minor stroke last year—I know it scared Owen and made him decide to slow down and spend more time with her."

"When did you know?" he asked again.

She moved back to the stove, turned the chicken. "The beginning of August."

More than a month ago—and she hadn't told him.

He knew how much she loved her job, how disappointed she must have been to learn that the company was selling out to a competitor and yet she'd never said a single word to him about it.

He took a bottle of water from the fridge, twisted the cap off, took a long swallow. "Was it before or after you agreed to marry me?"

She folded her arms across the chest. "Where are you going with this, Craig?"

"Before or after?" he asked again.

"Before," she admitted.

He nodded then tipped the bottle to his mouth again. Her response confirmed what he'd suspected—what he'd feared.

"Well, that explains why you suddenly did a one-eighty in your attitude about marriage. Within the space of a few weeks you were hit by the realization that you were pregnant, losing your apartment and soon to be unemployed. I can understand that you were feeling desperate." He gripped the bottle so tightly he cracked the plastic. He tossed it into the sink. "Desperate enough to marry me."

Tess stared at him. "You think I married you because I was losing my job?"

"Well, there was never any doubt that I'd be able to support you and the baby, was there?"

Her eyes narrowed, flashed with anger. But her voice, when she spoke, was carefully controlled. "I didn't marry you for your bank account."

"Then why did you marry me?" he demanded.

"Because I'm in love with you, you idiot."

* * *

The only response to Tess's declaration was sudden and complete silence.

Craig stared at her, clearly stunned—and obviously terrified. She should have expected such a reaction. Nothing unnerved him more than talk of messy emotions.

She turned back to the pan on the stove. "I probably should have found a better way to say those words for the first time."

Out of the corner of her eye, she saw him take a step back, a physical retreat that reinforced the emotional withdrawal she'd already glimpsed in his eyes.

"I don't need or want such declarations," he said coolly.

And her heart broke just a little bit more.

She dumped rice into the pot of boiling water, covered it with a lid. "Maybe you don't," she agreed softly. "But maybe I needed to finally tell you how I feel because keeping it bottled up inside certainly hasn't made it go away."

"This wasn't in the plan, Tess."

"Yeah, well, it caught me off guard, too."

He frowned at that.

"Do you think I wanted this? How do you think it makes me feel, being in love with a man who obviously doesn't feel the same way about me?"

"You know I care about you, Tess."

She swallowed around the lump in her throat. "Yes, I do know that."

Neither of them seemed to know what to say after that and a long moment passed before Craig spoke again. "I'm going to check in at the lab."

Tess only nodded.

He walked out.

She stood there for several minutes after he'd gone, trying to understand how the marriage that had started out so promising could, just one month later, already be falling apart.

She should have told him about her job—she knew that. But she'd had valid reasons for keeping the news to herself for the present. At least, they'd seemed valid at the time. Now, obviously, she recognized the mistake in not telling him from the outset.

But how could she have guessed that he would jump to such conclusions? And how could he believe she would marry him for his money—especially when he was the one who had bullied her into this marriage?

Okay, that wasn't a fair statement to make. She'd gone into this marriage with her eyes open accepting the terms he'd offered. It was her own fault for expecting more—for hoping he might one day fall in love with her as she'd fallen in love with him.

It wasn't until she smelled it burning that she remembered she'd left dinner on the stove. She dumped the charred chicken and scorched rice into the sink, thinking that Laurie was wrong.

She had managed to screw this up, too.

Chapter Twelve

It was almost five hours later before Craig came home again.

Tess had put her pajamas on and tried to sleep, but after tossing and turning for longer than she wanted to admit she finally got up to make herself a cup of peppermint tea. She had just settled down at the table with it when he got back.

"I overreacted to the news about your job," he said. "It just caught me off guard, to hear it from Owen rather than you."

"I should have told you," she admitted softly. "But I wanted to have another job lined up first. I didn't want you to think that you had to find something at Richmond for me."

"I've been thinking about that," he admitted. "And I

know it doesn't require a computer science degree, but we have an opening—"

"I'll find another job," she interrupted. "But thank you."

"I'm trying to apologize here, Tess."

"It's really not necessary." She stood up, carried her cup to the sink to dump the tea. "We each had our own reasons for agreeing to this marriage, I shouldn't be surprised that you wondered about mine."

His, on the other hand, had been clear from the outset—to give their baby the stability of a two-parent family, no emotional commitment required or even desired.

She felt his hands on her shoulders and stiffened instinctively. He stilled and she thought for a moment he might pull away. But he slid his hands down her arms and around her, drawing her back against the hard length of his body.

She wanted to stay mad—she was definitely still hurting. But she was scared that if she let this issue come between them, they wouldn't get past it, so she closed her eyes and let herself relax against him.

His hand splayed over the slight bulge of her tummy, rubbed gently. The tenderness of the gesture was at odds with his earlier antagonism—or maybe it wasn't. Because she was finally realizing that his feelings for her were completely separate from his feelings for their baby.

The baby was the reason he'd married her—she wouldn't let herself forget that again. But she couldn't stop loving him just because he refused to love her and she couldn't give up the hope that her love would help him open his heart.

Without giving herself time to think she turned in his arms and lifted her mouth to his.

He might have been caught off guard at first but he quickly overcame his surprise to take control of the kiss. His mouth moved over hers in a slow sensual glide that made everything inside her quiver and melt. Then his tongue dipped inside, stroking hers in a slow, lazy dance of seduction and the heat in her belly spread until her whole body felt as though it was on fire.

He scooped her into his arms and carried her to the bedroom.

Passion flared quickly, burned hotly. Their bodies were attuned to each other now and moved together effortlessly. Her climax came easily, wave after wave rushing over her, sweeping her away on a seemingly endless tide of pleasure that soon carried him along with it.

It was several more minutes before their breathing had leveled and their bodies had cooled. When Craig lifted himself away from her she shivered with the chill, finally accepting that the physical closeness they shared could never compensate for the emotional intimacy she needed.

"Craig…"

He smoothed her hair away from her face, kissed her softly. "Please don't complicate this, Tess."

Maybe she should have let it go, but she couldn't. "Don't you want more?"

"What we have between us is real and good—why can't that be enough?"

"I don't know," she admitted softly. "I only know that it's not."

His eyes were filled with sadness and regret as he

trailed his fingertips down her cheek. "I'm sorry I can't give you what you need."

"So am I," she said softly.

Then she rolled onto her side, turning away from him so he wouldn't see the tears in her eyes.

Tess debated over her decision for several days before she made the call, wanting to make sure she wasn't acting impulsively. If she was going to justify her decision—and she knew she would have to—she needed to know that it was based on logic and reason rather than emotion. It was hard, though, to remove her feelings from the equation when she was still hurt by Craig's accusations and his dismissal of her feelings.

Her conversation with Jared McCabe was brief but when she hung up she was relieved that she'd at least taken a step forward. Now she only had to talk to Craig about her decision.

She knew his department was launching a new drug trial this weekend and he'd left a message on the machine earlier warning that he would be late. She understood that he liked to be on hand to ensure there were no snags early on but she hadn't expected that he would be this late. She wondered if they'd run into some problems—or if he was just avoiding her.

Pushing the thought out of her mind, she got ready for bed. She brushed her teeth and settled in with a book, determined to wait up for him to get home.

She stayed awake until after midnight, then finally fell asleep facing the empty side of the bed.

Craig woke up desperately wanting a shower and coffee, not necessarily in that order. So when he caught a whiff of his favorite French Roast in the air, he followed the scent into the kitchen. His eyes were gritty from lack of sleep, his jaw was in desperate need of a razor and his clothes were rumpled from being slept in.

Tess, on the other hand, looked bright and fresh sitting at the table reading the paper. "I made real coffee this morning—I figured you could use it."

He nodded as he made his way to the cupboard for a mug. "Thanks."

She waited while he filled his mug and took a long sip. It was hot and strong and the jolt of caffeine cleared some of the fog around his brain.

"I didn't hear you come in last night," she said.

There was no censure in her voice, only concern. But he felt the weight of guilt anyway, conscious of the fact that he could have called—should have called. But things had been tense between them since their argument about Tess losing her job and everything that came after and he'd taken the easy way, leaving a message on the machine at home when he knew she was still at work, trusting that she would track him down at the lab if she needed anything.

Because of that guilt, or maybe just because he wanted to make an effort to get their relationship back on track, he carried his mug to the table and sat down across from her.

"It was early this morning," he admitted. "I didn't want to disturb you so I crashed on the sofa."

"Did you run into problems with the trial?"

He nodded. "Some idiot lied on his intake form about

a medication he was taking and within half an hour of dosing, he was vomiting all over the place."

"The drug didn't show up on his prescreen blood work?"

"He wasn't taking it then. Apparently he came down with some kind of bronchial infection last week, went to his doctor to get something for it because he didn't want to be cut from the study.

"We're lucky it was a relatively mild drug interaction but Kaitlyn had to take him to the hospital to be checked out, leaving the rest of us to work on damage control while still trying to keep the study on schedule. Thankfully there were no other complications, at least not while I was still there."

"Sounds like it was a rough night," she said sympathetically.

He nodded again.

"Did you want some breakfast?" she asked. "I've already had mine, but I could—"

"No, thanks," he interrupted, feeling even more guilty that she was being so considerate when his own actions had been so thoughtless. "I'm just going to have another cup of coffee and grab a shower before I head back."

"Oh."

He finished his coffee in one long swallow and stood up to get a refill.

He glanced over at Tess, saw that she was staring at the paper but not reading. There was obviously something on her mind, something he instinctively suspected he didn't want to get into—not in his current sleep-deprived state, anyway—but he felt compelled to ask, "What are you thinking about?"

"I wanted to talk to you," she admitted. "But I didn't want to dump it on you like this."

"What is it?"

"I'm leaving for San Diego tomorrow."

"San Diego? What are you talking about?"

"I've been offered a short-term contract at GigaPix."

He couldn't have been more stunned if she'd stood up on the table and started dancing.

It had been eight days since they'd argued about Tess losing her job and though things had been a little awkward between them since then, he'd honestly thought they would soon be back to the way things used to be. He sure as hell hadn't bargained on something like this.

"You said you loved me."

"My decision to go to San Diego doesn't have anything to do with my feelings for you."

He didn't believe her. "Then why are you doing this? Why now?"

"Because I realized that, despite my qualifications, no one's going to want to hire a woman who will be taking maternity leave in a few months and because Jared needs some help finishing up the program I'd been working on at SBG."

"You don't need to work, Tess. I can afford—"

"No," she interrupted sharply. "It's not about how much you're worth, it's about my self-worth. I won't let you believe that my marriage to you was some kind of retirement plan—"

"I know it wasn't."

She looked at him skeptically. "Do you?"

"Of course. I was just surprised to find out about SBG and I reacted without thinking." He realized it was the closest he'd come to actually apologizing for the accusations he'd made and he could tell by the look on Tess's face that it was too little too late.

"In any event," she continued. "The money Jared is offering will more than compensate for the time I'll need to be off with the baby."

"Don't do this, Tess."

"It's only for six weeks," she said.

Six weeks sounded like forever to him and he was suddenly, desperately afraid that if she left, she would never come back.

"We hit a rough spot, Tess. Every marriage goes through periods of adjustment. How are we going to work through it if you run away?"

"I'm not running," she said. "Although I won't deny that I need some time away and Jared's offer seemed like the perfect opportunity to take it."

He gulped a mouthful of hot coffee, barely felt the burn. "I'm not giving you a divorce."

She seemed genuinely startled by his statement. "I'm not asking for a divorce, I'm only asking for six weeks."

Except she wasn't really asking and they both knew it. She'd made up her mind and he could either acquiesce or argue with her but it wouldn't change her decision.

"You've made the arrangements already," he guessed.

She nodded.

"Then I guess this discussion is over."

Tess didn't ask Craig to take her to the airport and he didn't offer. He didn't want her to go and there was no way in hell he was going to make it easier for her. But when he got up Sunday morning he saw her suitcases standing in the hallway beside the front door, mocking him like twin exclamation marks at the end of a sentence: You blew it!! And he felt a kind of helpless anguish he couldn't ever remember feeling and didn't know what to do about.

He found her in the kitchen, writing a note.

Had she planned on leaving without even saying goodbye to him?

"I was just jotting down the address and phone number of where I'll be staying in San Diego in case you need to reach me," she said. "And there's a copy of my itinerary on the fridge."

He took the sticky note she offered, noted the residential address. "I thought you'd be staying in a hotel."

She shook her head. "I don't even want to imagine what a hotel would cost for six weeks."

"Whose place is this?" he asked.

"Jared's sister's. She's a singer in some country band and is on tour in Europe for a few months so I'm subletting her apartment."

He nodded, as if it was okay. As if the idea of his wife moving halfway across the country to live in a stranger's home was even remotely acceptable to him.

She glanced at her watch. "My cab's going to be here in a few minutes."

He followed her to the living room, where she stood by the window to wait for her ride. He didn't want her going away with so much still unresolved between them. He didn't want her going away at all. But he didn't know what to say—he didn't know if there was anything he could say—to change her mind. "Tess…"

She turned around, one hand holding the edge of the curtain, waiting.

But he seemed at a complete loss for words, and she'd already said everything there was to say.

Then she heard the beep of a horn.

"My ride's here."

"Wait." He took her hands, held on for a long moment.

She waited again, her throat tight and her eyes burning, knowing she was a fool for even letting herself hope he might say the three little words she so desperately wanted to hear.

Despite all the reasons she'd enumerated for accepting the six-week contract in California, she knew that if he said those three words, she'd call Jared McCabe in a heartbeat and cancel her trip.

"Don't go, Tess."

Three words—but not quite the ones she needed.

She drew a deep breath and stepped away. "I have to."

Then, before she could change her mind, she picked up her suitcases and walked out the door.

Craig had barely slept since Tess had been gone.

No matter how many times he changed the sheets, he could still smell her scent on her pillow—a scent that haunted him with memories of all the nights they'd lain there together and taunted him with her absence.

He tried sleeping in one of the spare rooms and even on the sofa, but it didn't make any difference. He wanted to be in his bed with Tess.

There wasn't anywhere he could go in the house without thoughts of her intruding. But it wasn't just in the house, it was everywhere he went. It seemed that not more than an hour passed on any given day without him thinking about her, wondering what she was doing, missing her.

It was strange how easily he'd adapted to her presence and how difficult it was to adapt to her absence.

They spoke on the telephone almost every day but he usually initiated the calls and their conversations were always cordial but short, as if neither of them knew what to say to the other.

So when his brother showed up at the house on Wednesday night in the third week of Tess's absence, Craig was grateful for the distraction.

Until Gage asked, "Where's your wife tonight?"

Craig hadn't told his family about her six-week contract in California because he didn't want to talk about it. As if by not discussing it, he could pretend she wasn't really gone.

"In San Diego," he admitted.

"Business trip?"

"Yeah." It was the simplest, if not the complete, answer.

"Well, at least now I know why you've been so surly," his brother noted. "When's she going to be back?"

"The middle of November."

Gage frowned. "That's a long trip."

Twenty-five more days, Craig knew, though he was hardly going to admit to his brother that he was counting.

But Gage's eyes narrowed thoughtfully. "You're obviously not giving me the whole story."

Craig shrugged, as if his wife's absence was inconsequential. "She was offered a six-week contract at GigaPix and she decided it was too good an opportunity to pass up."

"And you just let her go?" he asked incredulously.

"It wasn't my choice to make."

"Okay, then," Gage allowed. "What did you do to make her want to leave for six weeks?"

"What makes you think I had anything to do with it?" he challenged aware that he sounded just a little defensive.

"The fact that you've barely been married two months and you're here alone and looking miserable."

He sighed. "You're right—I screwed up. I found out that Tess knew she was losing her job before we got engaged and basically accused her of marrying me for my bank account."

"Well, that would do it." Gage shook his head, obviously disgusted by his brother's idiocy. "Where would you ever come up with an idea like that?"

"It's why Lana wanted to marry me."

"You're not seriously comparing Tess to that piranha." His brother sounded as indignant as Tess had been.

"I had a momentary lapse."

"No wonder she's pissed at you."

Craig started to defend his position, then realized there really was no defense. Because he knew Tess and he should have known that she would never use him. Then again, he'd never thought she would leave him after they'd exchanged wedding vows, either. But here he was and she was gone.

She'd said she loved him, yet she'd walked away without so much as a backward glance.

It's only six weeks.

But it was more than that. To Craig, it was further

proof that no one had ever loved him enough to stay. Not his mother or Lana. Not even Tess.

And that realization might have bothered him far more than anything else—if he hadn't learned a long time ago to lock down his emotions.

Tess had been working fourteen hours a day since she got to California, partly because she was anxious to get the DirectorPlus Five program up and running, but mostly because she needed to focus on something other than the mess she'd already made of her marriage. And so, by the end of her third week, only halfway through the term of her contract, she finished upgrading the program.

She didn't tell Jared right away, because she wanted to run it through some test exercises, checking for flaws and gaps before she turned it over. Which was why he found her at her desk Saturday morning when she'd been given explicit instructions to take the weekend off.

"You're going to make me look bad—working longer hours than the boss."

She continued tapping away at the keyboard, her eyes on the screen. "I should have warned you that I can become a little obsessive when I get started on something."

"Aren't pregnant women supposed to rest?"

"I've been sitting in front of a computer, not climbing mountains with a fifty-pound pack on my back."

"I know I should probably be thanking you rather than complaining," Jared said. "But I'm worried that you're pushing yourself too hard."

"I'm not," she said. "And I'm done."

He frowned. "What?"

She turned to look at him and smiled. "I'm done."

As realization dawned, the confusion on his face gave way to sheer delight. "It's really finished?"

"Yep."

"But you're weeks ahead of schedule. My programmers said it would take at least six weeks to get it up and running."

"Your programmers weren't as familiar with the software as I am," she reminded him.

"Can I play with it?" he asked, sounding as excited as a child with a new toy.

Tess laughed and pushed away from the desk so Jared could get to the computer.

Several minutes passed while he put the software through its paces, then he turned back to her. "Wow."

She smiled again. "It's great, isn't it?"

"This calls for a celebration," he decided.

"What did you have in mind?"

"Getting you out of this office, for starters," he said. "Have you seen anything of the city since you arrived?"

"Only what's between here and your sister's apartment," she admitted.

"Then we definitely need to do something about that."

She wasn't sure what he had in mind and was pleasantly surprised when he took her to the zoo.

"This is amazing." Tess stared at the park map in her hand trying to figure out which way to go, what she wanted to see first. "I had no idea it was so big."

"A hundred acres in the middle of the city," Jared told her. "With about four thousand animals here—and more than seven hundred thousand plants."

"I want to see everything," she said.

He laughed. "Well, the zoo closes at five, but we could always come back another day."

"Actually, I've already booked my flight to go home," she told him. "Now that the program's finished, there's no reason for me to stay."

"I guess you're anxious to get back," he said.

She nodded. Though she'd had work to keep her busy through the days, she'd found the nights unbearably lonely. She'd missed Craig—talking with him, laughing with him, even arguing with him. But mostly she missed going to sleep beside him at night and waking with his arms around her in the morning.

Not for the first time, she wondered if she'd taken the coward's way out—jumping at the chance to come to San Diego rather than staying in Pinehurst and fighting it out with Craig. But she'd been so angry he could think—even for a moment—that she'd marry him for his money and she'd been devastated when he'd walked out after the declaration of her true feelings—blatantly rejecting her love.

"Let's start at the Reptile House," Jared suggested, interrupting her wayward thoughts.

Tess shuddered. "Let's not."

"You said you wanted to see everything," he reminded her.

She glanced at the map. "Let's start with the koalas and kangaroos," she said, noting that those exhibit areas were on the opposite side of the park.

"All right," he agreed. "We'll start with the koalas and kangaroos."

They worked their way around the north side of the park and circled back toward the Giant Panda Research

Station, stopping for ice cream after Tess had used almost a whole roll of film taking pictures of Hua Mei and the other black-and-white bears.

She was glad for the rest. Having spent the better part of the last three weeks behind a desk in a climate-controlled office, the muscles in her legs were protesting the vigorous workout and the unaccustomed heat.

Tess finished her double scoop of orange-pineapple sherbet and wiped her fingers on a paper napkin. "Next stop: Polar Bear Plunge."

"Ready when you are," Jared said, offering his hand to help her up from the bench.

She accepted and was glad she had because when she stood up she almost fell down again.

He moved closer, grabbing for her other hand to keep her upright. "What's wrong?"

"I don't know," she said. "I just felt light-headed all of a sudden."

He gently guided her back onto the bench. "Sit for a minute."

"I've been sitting," she reminded him.

"Yeah, but it won't hurt you to sit some more."

So she did and the dizziness passed. Mostly, anyway.

"Okay?" he asked after several minutes.

She nodded.

He helped her to her feet again. "I think we should call it a day."

"But we haven't seen the monkeys," she felt compelled to point out.

"We've seen enough for today."

"Okay," she agreed, because she was ready to go.

Jared cranked up the air conditioning in his car as

they drove out of the parking lot and Tess leaned back and closed her eyes. She wasn't aware that she'd fallen asleep until Jared shook her awake when they arrived at the hospital.

Chapter Thirteen

Tess wanted to be annoyed with Jared for not consulting her before deciding she needed to see a doctor but the truth was, she was glad to be there. Though she didn't want to express her concerns aloud she knew she'd feel a lot better after she'd been checked over and reassured that everything was okay.

Except that when she excused herself to go to the bathroom while waiting for her exam, she found her underpants spotted with bright red blood and knew that everything wasn't going to be okay.

"The problem seems to be a low-lying placenta," Dr. Smye told her, after he'd reviewed the report from her ultrasound.

She swallowed. "What does that mean?"

"What it means for you right now is that you get to spend the night here. The bleeding wasn't heavy and it stopped on its own and that's a good sign. Your baby is measuring right where he should for twenty-two weeks and is active, which is another good sign. But bleeding at any stage is a concern and could be an indication that you'll have trouble maintaining your pregnancy."

She didn't want to ask the question, wasn't sure she wanted to know, but she found herself saying, "What do you mean?"

The doctor looked at her with kindness and compassion in his weary eyes. "It means that you might lose this baby."

And the panic that she'd been trying to hold at bay since she discovered the bleeding suddenly closed in on her from all sides making her eyes sting, her throat burn and her heart ache.

"No." Tess shook her head as she spoke around the tightness in her throat. "I can't lose this baby."

"I can't promise you that you won't," Dr. Smye said.

His tone was somehow both gentle and matter-of-fact, indicating that he'd seen this condition before, spoken these words before. But his experience and expertise didn't reassure Tess because this time it was her baby he was talking about.

"It's simply too early to tell," the doctor continued. "For now, we can only hope that you won't experience any more bleeding and that the placenta will move away from the cervix. But your own doctor will want to monitor that with regular ultrasounds every three to four weeks for the duration of your pregnancy."

Tess silently vowed that she would do everything she could, everything Dr. Bowen told her to do to keep her baby safe.

After the doctor was finished with her, Jared came back into the examining room.

"I called your husband," he told her.

She dropped her head back against the pillows and closed her eyes.

"Don't you think he'd want to know?"

"Of course," she admitted. "But now he'll feel obligated to drop everything and come out here…"

"His flight will be in at eleven," Jared confirmed.

"Was he…was he very angry?"

"Angry?" He frowned. "Why would you think he'd be angry?"

"Aside from the fact that he didn't want me coming out here in the first place?"

Jared hesitated, as if considering his words. "I don't know you all that well and I don't know what the situation is between you and your husband," he said at last. "But I do know that the man I spoke to on the phone was deeply concerned about you, Tess."

"Because of the baby," she said softly. And she was concerned about their baby, too, but she still couldn't help wishing that Craig cared as much about her.

He sat in the chair beside her bed. "Did you marry him because you were pregnant?"

She shook her head. "No, but he only proposed because I was pregnant."

"I wouldn't be so sure of that."

But she was. She'd hoped Craig would grow to love her, but the way he'd reacted when she told him she loved him confirmed that she'd been harboring a futile hope. He didn't now and never would love her.

"He married me to give our baby a family," she admitted. "That's all that matters to Craig."

"Obviously, you have reasons for believing that," Jared said. "But you should know that when I talked to him, he only asked about *you*—he never even mentioned the baby."

Throughout the six-hour flight to San Diego, Craig couldn't stop thinking about Tess. It seemed like the longest flight he'd ever taken. And then the cab ride from the airport to the hospital seemed to take forever all over again.

By the time he arrived at Memorial Hospital in San Diego, almost ten hours had passed since Jared McCabe's phone call. So much could happen in that period of time and his heart was in his throat as he rode the elevator to the fifth floor. And then he had to stop at the nurses' station to find out what room Tess was in because he'd forgot to get that information on the phone.

It was almost midnight by then and he half expected someone would try to turn him away. But whether the nurse read the determination in his face or felt sorry for him because he was so obviously rumpled and weary with exhaustion, she led him to Tess's room.

"She's sleeping now but you can go in to check on her—for your own peace of mind. Then I'd suggest you find a hotel for the night and come back in the morning."

"I want to stay."

She shrugged, clearly not intending to fight him on the issue and pushed open the door for him to enter.

He tiptoed quietly into the room, his steps almost faltering when he saw Tess. She looked so fragile and pale in the narrow hospital bed, her rounded belly covered by a thin sheet, an IV tube in the back of her hand.

In all the years he'd known her, she'd rarely been sick even with something as simple as a common cold. She'd always been healthy and strong, almost invincible. But she looked fragile and vulnerable right now, and he wanted nothing more than to take her in his arms and protect her.

Except that it was his fault she was here. If he hadn't pushed Tess about losing her job at SBG, she never would have come out here to work for Jared and she wouldn't be lying in this hospital bed right now.

He knew he didn't deserve her forgiveness, but as he bent down to touch his lips to her forehead, he silently prayed that she'd give it to him, anyway.

Her eyelids fluttered, then opened slowly. "Craig?"

"Shh," he said softly. "They'll kick me out of here if they find out I woke you."

"I wasn't really sleeping," she admitted.

"You should be," he said.

"So should you. It's—" her eyes darted to the clock on the wall across from her bed "—3:00 a.m. your time."

Your time—as if they were from different worlds. And suddenly he felt the distance of those three time zones like an unbridgeable chasm between them.

No, he refused to believe that the thoughtless words he'd spoken to her more than three weeks ago could create such distance between them. This was Tess—his best friend, his wife, the mother of his child. And he was going to fight to keep her.

He lowered himself into one of the ugly vinyl-covered chairs beside the bed. He reached for her free hand and wasn't surprised to see that his own was shaking. His entire system had been a jumble of quivering nerves since he'd received Jared's telephone call.

He brushed her hair away from her face, noted the dark circles under her eyes, the pallor of her skin. "How are you?"

"I'm okay. A little scared, but okay." She squeezed his hand. "I'm glad you're here."

And those last few words made all the difference to him. Throughout the trip from New York, he'd wondered whether he was doing the right thing, whether Tess would be happy to see him or resent his presence. Now, some of the tightness around his chest finally eased.

"I wasn't sure, after the way things were between us when I left—"

"You said you wanted some time," he reminded her. "I was giving you time."

She nodded, then moved her hand to her tummy.

"What's wrong?" he asked immediately. "Do you need the doctor?"

"No, I'm okay," she said, and guided his hand to the side of her belly.

He immediately felt a series of little vibrations through the taut skin.

"Is that—" he cleared his throat, which suddenly felt tight.

She nodded, her eyes shining with excitement. "That's our baby," she confirmed.

He felt the baby move again.

"The doctor said I could lose the baby," she admitted softly, staring through tear-filled eyes at his hand covering their baby. "I can't let myself even think about it—especially when I feel him moving like this, inside of me and know that he's depending on me…"

It was a possibility he'd forced himself to consider on the long trip west and one he'd been glad not to have to face. At least not yet.

He brushed a tear off her cheek. "You're doing everything you can to take care of our baby, Tess. That's all you can do."

And then, hoping to take some of the sadness from her eyes, he said, "I notice you still seem to be stuck on 'he'."

"Well, the ultrasound technician thought he was a he."

He kept his hand on her belly, savoring the skin-on-skin contact after having been apart from her for so long.

She'd only been gone half of the six weeks she'd intended but he knew—from his conversation with Jared—that she'd finished the program and had intended to come home. He'd learned something else from Jared and he asked her about that now.

"Why didn't you tell me that you'd been offered a permanent position at GigaPix?"

"Because I had no intention of accepting it."

"But why?" That was another question he'd been mulling over since the software company CEO had told him about his initial offer. He knew how much she loved her job and how hard it would be for her to find anything else comparable to what GigaPix could offer her.

"Because I'm having your baby," she reminded him. "And if I moved three thousand miles away, you would hardly ever see him."

"You turned down the job so I could be part of our baby's life?"

"So we could be a family," she said.

He was stunned by the admission and humbled by what she was offering. But mostly he was ashamed that he'd accused her of using him to get what she wanted when she'd been putting his wants ahead of her own all along.

"Is that still what you want?" he asked gently.

He hadn't realized he was holding his breath waiting for her response until he finally released it when she nodded.

"Does that mean you'll come home with me?"

"As soon as they let me out of here," she promised.

Tess and Craig returned from San Diego on Tuesday. Grace managed to hold off until Thursday before stopping by for a visit with her daughter-in-law.

She was surprised, but not displeased, when the door was answered by a woman who introduced herself as Irene Chambers—a retired nurse hired by Mr. Richmond to take care of the house and meals and look after his wife. Grace knew how important this baby was to her son and she was glad to see that he was taking such good care of his wife.

Irene showed Grace into the living room, where Tess was sitting with her feet up flipping through the pages of a parenting magazine, then excused herself to make tea.

Tess immediately closed the book when Grace stepped into the room, her eyes lighting up with pleasure. "This is a wonderful surprise," she said.

"I would have been here sooner," Grace admitted, "but Craig asked me to give you some time to settle in."

"If I was any more settled, I'd be a fixture," Tess told her.

She chuckled as she sat down on the other end of the couch, but with her back against the arm so that she was facing her daughter-in-law. "How are you feeling?"

"Good. I saw Dr. Bowen this morning and the baby—"

"I didn't ask about the baby," Grace interrupted gently. "I asked about you."

"Oh," Tess said.

And she sounded so surprised Grace wondered if she'd lost all sense of herself through the course of her pregnancy and she made a mental note to slap her son for allowing that to happen.

"I'm good," her daughter-in-law responded to the question at last and left it at that.

She sighed. "I love both of my sons, but that doesn't mean I'm blind to their faults. And I know something had to have happened between you and Craig for you to take off for San Diego the way you did."

"A misunderstanding."

"Is that a diplomatic way of saying that he reacted first and asked questions later?"

"It doesn't matter now," Tess said.

"Of course it does," Grace said, even though she appreciated Tess's loyalty to her husband. "I know you're both concerned about the baby, but I can't help feeling there's more going on."

"He wasn't happy about my decision to go to California," Tess admitted.

"Although I'm sure he was somehow instrumental in that decision."

Tess was silent for a moment before she said, "We had an argument about our reasons for getting married, I told him I loved him and he walked out."

"I'm sorry."

"But you're not surprised," her daughter-in-law guessed.

No, Grace wasn't surprised. Disappointed that he was still carrying around such old baggage, but not surprised.

"Craig hasn't had an easy go of it with women and emotions," she explained. "His mother played a lot of head games with both of the boys—giving and withdrawing affection as suited her moods. Gage, thankfully, was too young to really understand it. But Craig tried so hard to please her, with varying results and ultimately she rejected him completely when she chose her new husband over her children.

"Then there was Valerie—remember the girl he dated through his senior year of high school?"

Tess nodded.

"She and Craig had planned to go to the same college, but she decided to go to Notre Dame instead of Princeton. I have no doubt it was the right choice for her and even if she'd gone to Princeton, their high school romance wouldn't have survived the pressures and changes of college life. But Craig took her decision as another personal rejection.

"Then, of course, there was Lana. You know what a number she did on him."

"But he should know me well enough to know that I would never use my feelings against him," Tess protested.

"And yet, didn't you do exactly that?" she asked gently.

Tess looked startled. "What do you mean?"

"You told him you loved him and when he couldn't give the words back to you, you left."

"I didn't do it to hurt him. I did it because I needed something to focus on so *I* would stop hurting."

Grace nodded. "I'm not saying you were wrong to go. I'm only trying to help you understand how it probably looked to Craig."

"I do love him," Tess said. "He makes me angry and frustrated and crazy sometimes, but I love him."

"I know you do," she assured her. "And deep inside, he knows it, too."

Tess's eyes filled with tears and she dropped her gaze. "Do you think…" She hesitated, then shook her head.

But Grace already knew what she was thinking. She heard the question she didn't ask as clearly as if she'd spoken it aloud. "Do I think he could ever love you?"

Tess shook her head again. "It's a crazy thought."

"Oh, Tess. It's not crazy at all." Grace reached over and squeezed her hand gently. "But you're getting hung up on the words, honey. I'm not denying that they're important, but you need to stop listening to what he's not saying and start reading what he does."

Tess looked puzzled.

"Maybe it's a mental block with him, but just because he isn't saying the words doesn't mean he doesn't love you."

The period from Thanksgiving through to Christmas was usually Tess's favorite time of year. She loved to decorate and bake and shop and wrap. This year, however, her activity was severely restricted by doctor's orders and her own concerns about her baby, leaving Tess dependent upon others to assist with the tasks she enjoyed so much.

And despite her concerns, everything got done. Mrs. Chambers had taken care of the baking, although she let Tess sit at the table in the kitchen for a couple of hours each afternoon to help ice the sugar cookies. Grace and Allan and even Gage, had come around to help put up the decorations, wrapping garland around banisters, hanging wreaths and bows, setting Tess's collection of nutcrackers on the mantle of the fireplace. Laurie had taken care of most of her shopping and the wrapping, allowing Tess to write the tags and stick on the bows but nothing more strenuous than that.

But the highlight of the holiday preparations for Tess was when Craig took her to get the tree—just the two of them.

It was a crisp, clear day and the ground was covered in a thin blanket of fresh snow. Because he worried that the ground might be slippery, he kept her hand tucked in the crook of his arm as they slowly made their way up and down the rows of spruce and balsam and pine in search of the perfect specimen. And when they'd found it, he'd settled her down on a nearby stump to watch as he wielded his axe in battle against the blue spruce.

When the tree finally toppled, he turned to her with a look of such triumphant joy in his eyes and a smile of such pure joy on his face that her heart stuttered. She loved his boyish enthusiasm and his ability to find pleasure in the simplest things and she knew that he was going to be a terrific father to their child.

He struggled to get a grip on the trunk, then dragged the tree over to where she was sitting.

"Our first Christmas tree," he'd said proudly.

She smiled and nodded but she couldn't help wondering if their first would also be their last. She knew they both wanted this marriage to work but she also knew that they couldn't go on forever as they'd been going the last several weeks.

The distance between them was her own fault. He hadn't wanted her to go to California, but she'd gone anyway. Her pride had demanded it. There was no way she could stay in Pinehurst, unemployed, after he'd compared her to Lana. She'd needed to go to San Diego to prove that she could still support herself, that she wasn't looking for a free ride. Except that she wasn't capable of supporting herself right now, and though it was by circumstance rather than choice, she wondered if Craig resented her dependence on him.

It took a great deal more wrestling to get the tree strapped onto the top of his car and then unstrapped again and set up in their living room. But once that was all done, he actually let her help decorate it—although he kept a close eye on her to ensure she didn't do too much reaching or bending. And afterward, he popped a bowl of popcorn and they sat together on the sofa, snacking and drinking hot chocolate and watching the lights twinkle.

"What do you think?" he asked.

"It's perfect," she assured him. And though it was a little lopsided and a couple of the branches had broken when Craig maneuvered it into the house, it was perfect to Tess.

The baby kicked hard, demanding she pay attention to him instead of the tree and she smiled as she laid her hand on her belly to assure him that he hadn't been forgotten.

Craig put his hand beside hers and rubbed gently. He'd been touching her belly a lot recently, fascinated by the baby's seemingly constant activity.

"Can you believe that by this time next year he'll be sitting here with us?" he asked.

"By this time next year, he probably won't be doing much sitting at all," Tess said. "He'll be crawling around, trying to pull ornaments off of the tree and tear bows off of presents."

"Now who's been reading up on child care?" he teased.

"Well, I have to do something while I'm under house arrest."

"Bed rest," he corrected mildly.

"Same thing."

"I can understand why you're feeling frustrated."

"I'm not really frustrated," she said. "Because I know I'm doing what's best for the baby. But I am starting to get bored. It seems that all I do is sit around reading or watching reruns of *CSI*."

"Maybe we could find you a hobby."

"I tried knitting," she admitted.

"You knit?" The surprise was evident in his voice.

"No, I don't knit," she said irritably. "I said I *tried.*"

He chuckled. "I imagine your attempt lasted all of about three minutes."

"Four," she disputed.

"Well, it won't be too much longer before you'll have our baby to keep you busy."

"I know." And it was that thought which kept her off her feet when she desperately wanted to be doing something. "And your mom and my sister have been stopping by frequently—whether to keep me company or keep an eye on me, I'm not sure, but I appreciate having someone around to talk to."

"Speaking of my mother," he said. "She dropped by this morning with a fresh pine wreath for the front door and some mistletoe."

"Mistletoe?"

He smiled. "Not very subtle, is she?"

Tess couldn't disagree, but she knew that Grace was only trying to nudge her son and his wife closer together and she was touched—if a little embarrassed—by the gesture.

"What did you do with it?" she asked.

"I hung it up in the hall, where she'll be sure to see it the next time she visits."

She nodded.

"I thought about putting it over the couch," he said. "But then I decided that would be too obvious and I shouldn't need a leaf hanging overhead as an excuse to kiss my wife."

Tess didn't know what to say.

Was he suggesting that he did want to kiss her?

He hadn't done so in so long, she thought he'd lost complete interest. But the way he was looking at her now—as he hadn't looked at her in a very long time— made her feel all warm and tingly inside.

He brushed his thumb across her bottom lip in a slow, sensual motion. "Do I need an excuse?"

She swallowed. "Do you want to kiss me?"

"More than you can imagine," he said.

And then he *was* kissing her.

Tess's eyes drifted closed as his mouth moved over hers in a patiently masterful dance of seduction.

In everything else he did, he was decisive and purposeful—moving forward without hesitation. But when he kissed her, it was as if everything else faded away and they had all the time in the world.

He deepened the kiss slowly, gradually, as if giving her time to decide that this was what she wanted. It was definitely what she wanted.

His tongue glided over the seam of her lips, and she opened to welcome him. He dipped inside, teasing her with gentle strokes of his tongue. Oh, yeah, she wanted this. It seemed like forever since he'd kissed her like this and she only wanted it to go on forever.

She wished she could get closer to him; she wanted to feel the hard length of his body against her. But the mound of her belly made that impossible.

Then the baby kicked—hard.

She felt Craig's smile against her mouth, but still he kept kissing her, his hands moving down to her waist—or what had once been her waist—to caress the roundness of her belly. The baby kicked again, although less forcefully this time, then settled.

When he finally eased his lips from hers, she was breathless and dizzy—and she was pleased to note that he looked a little dazed himself.

He might have stopped kissing her, but he was still holding her in his arms, and for the first time since she'd returned from San Diego, she finally felt as though she was home.

"I've missed you so much, Tess."

She knew exactly what he meant, because although they'd been living together, even sharing the same bed, there had been a distance between them—the distance of suspicion and hurt that had driven a wedge between them since before she left for California. A distance that she knew they'd finally started to bridge.

"I've missed you, too," she admitted.

Maybe he wouldn't ever say the words she wanted to hear. Maybe he wouldn't ever love her the way she loved him. But she knew that he cared about her and was committed to their marriage and their family and that was enough for a fresh start.

Something changed between them after that kiss.

Craig wasn't sure exactly what or why, but he was grateful to see that some of the shadows had cleared from Tess's beautiful blue eyes. She smiled more frequently and laughed more easily and they grew closer and closer with each day that passed.

They had a wonderful Christmas together and spent time with each of their families over the holidays. They stayed at home on New Year's, sipping non-alcoholic champagne as they watched the celebration from Times Square on TV.

At her first check-up of the new year, Dr. Bowen confirmed that because the placenta was still covering the cervix, Tess would have to deliver the baby by caesarean section. She also ordered weekly ultrasounds to monitor the baby's development and ensure the procedure could be scheduled before Tess went into labor on her own.

Craig and Tess immediately began making serious

preparations for their baby's arrival. Because the doctor had ordered Tess to stay off of her feet, Craig got her a wheelchair so he could take her around to shop for furniture and little outfits and the million other things their baby would need. He brought home paint samples so they could pick the color for the nursery and he let her watch while he painted and set everything up. They had a lot of fun preparing for their baby's arrival, but more than that, they seemed to have rediscovered the joy of spending time with one another and simply being together. They no longer slept on opposite sides of the bed, but cuddled close together in the middle—or as close as they could get these days.

Craig had so much to be grateful for and so much more to look forward to and he was happier than he could ever remember being.

But did he love her?

That was the question that would often spring to mind when he found himself lying awake beside her in the night just watching her sleep.

He wanted to say that he did. He wanted to give her the words that he knew she wanted to hear. But as strong as his feelings for her were, he just didn't know. His affection for her was real and his commitment to their family unshakeable, and that—at least for him—as enough.

It was after midnight when Tess awoke, feeling achy and even more uncomfortable than usual. The baby was restless, too, kicking up a storm inside her belly.

She was still more than a month away from her actual due date, although at her doctor's appointment earlier that day, Dr. Bowen had scheduled her C-section for two days' time. She'd thought Tess could probably go another week to ten days further into her pregnancy with little risk but wanted to err on the side of caution. Tess was relieved she wouldn't have to carry so much extra weight around for very much longer. She imagined the baby would be relieved, too, to be released from his confinement. No doubt that's why he'd been so restless lately—there wasn't much room for him to move around in there anymore.

She felt a twinge in her lower back and rolled onto her other side hoping a change of position would ease the ache. The baby twisted around again, too, and now he was pressing directly on her bladder.

Tess got up to make a trip to the bathroom, then went downstairs to get a drink, frowning as the ache in her back seemed to worsen. She'd had cramps in her legs all day, too. Probably the strain from carrying the extra twenty pounds around. Or maybe she was stiff from lack of exercise. The further along she'd progressed in her pregnancy, the more the doctor—and Craig—had restricted her activities.

After about half an hour of walking, she thought the pain had started to ease. Or maybe she was just feeling too weak and weary to continue pacing the floors. Whatever the reason, she finally made her way back up to the bedroom, crawled under the covers and drifted into a restless sleep.

It was several hours later before she woke up again, gasping at the pain that ripped through her belly like a jagged knife.

* * *

When Craig returned to the bedroom after his morning shower, his initial surprise at finding his wife sitting up in bed was immediately superseded by deep, bone-chilling fear. It wasn't just that she was awake so early, it was the way her hands were fisted in the sheets, her brow crinkled in pain and the slow, shallow breaths that seemed to require all of her concentration.

"Tess?"

She turned her head, her eyes wide and slightly panicked. "I think…I'm in…labor."

Oh, no. Oh, Christ. Christ no. This was *not* supposed to be happening.

"You're not supposed to go into labor," he reminded her, as if maybe she'd just forgotten and could somehow miraculously put a halt to the process. "You have a C-section scheduled Thursday."

"Yeah, well…I guess we forgot…to tell…the baby," she joked weakly.

He forced away the panic, focused his thoughts. It wasn't going to do Tess any good if he fell apart.

"Okay," he said. "I'm going to help you get dressed, then we're going to call Dr. Bowen to meet us at the hospital."

"Okay," she agreed.

He found a pair of leggings and tunic top then dug through the drawer for a pair of warm socks. Tess's feet were always cold—it was a strange thought to be having in the moment, but maybe his mind needed to focus on something mundane because somehow holding those socks in his hand helped him to concentrate on what needed to be done.

But as he carried the clothes back over to the bed, he couldn't help remembering Doctor Bowen's warning to Tess: "if we let you go into labor on your own, it could be dangerous for both you and the baby."

He closed his eyes and said a quick and silent prayer that they would both be okay. After everything they'd been through already, he had to believe everything would be fine. He just had to get her dressed and to the hospital and then let the doctors take care of her.

He set the clothes on the bed and pulled back the sheets.

That's when he saw the blood.

Chapter Fourteen

After about two seconds' debate, Craig called an ambulance. And as he rode with Tess on the way to the hospital, he was glad he'd done so. He didn't understand all the medical jargon the paramedics tossed back and forth between themselves and over the radio, but he knew when they pulled out of the drive with the lights flashing and sirens screaming that Tess's condition wasn't good.

He held her hand tightly in his own as the medic set up an IV for a Ringers lactose infusion. Craig knew that Tess was in danger of going into shock and if she did—no, he wasn't going to allow himself to consider the possibility.

But she was so pale, and obviously in a lot of pain with the contractions that seemed to come with alarming frequency and increasing intensity.

"She's at thirty-four weeks," Craig told the para-

medic. "And scheduled to have a C-section Thursday.
Dr. Bowen's her OB-GYN."

"I don't think this baby's going to wait until Thursday," the paramedic responded. Then to his partner,
"Tell Memorial to call in Drs. Bowen and Greis to prep
for a priority one section."

It probably wasn't an unusual request, but there was
something in the other man's tone that alerted Craig.
"What's wrong?"

The paramedic gave a slight shake of his head.

"Tell me."

Tess must have picked up on his panic, because she
tried to push herself up. "The baby…?" It was all she
managed before she collapsed again when another pain
seized her.

Craig swallowed hard, squeezed her hand tighter.

"Relax, Mrs. Richmond. You're not going to help
your baby by fighting me. Let's just move you over on
to your side for a minute." As he spoke, he slid his arms
beneath her, helped turn to her gently. "We're going to
be at the hospital in a minute and a half."

But a minute and a half, Craig knew, could be
too late.

He heard the driver, still patched through to the hospital, relay the information given to him by his partner.

Tachycardia, the paramedic said, which Craig knew
was an abnormally rapid beating of the heart. Because
they monitored blood pressure and heart rates during
their trials in the lab, he knew that anything over one
hundred beats per minute at rest was considered fast
and Tess's rate was over one hundred and forty. Her
blood pressure, on the other hand, was dangerously

low because of the bleeding and he knew she was starting to fade.

"Craig." Her voice was growing weaker and her skin alarmingly pale.

"I'm here," he told her.

"Promise me…"

"Anything," he said hoarsely.

"Promise me you'll take care of our baby."

"Always."

Her eyes drifted shut. "If anything happens to me—"

"No," he interrupted, refusing to let her finish the thought. "Nothing's going to happen. Everything's going to be fine."

But she didn't hear him.

She'd already drifted into unconsciousness.

He thought he'd be relieved when they finally got to the hospital. And he was—until they whisked Tess away and directed him to a waiting room.

Dammit, he didn't want to be in a waiting room. He wanted to be with Tess.

But he needed to stay out of the way so the doctors could do their job—so they could save Tess and the baby.

Dr. Bowen had already started the emergency surgery and Dr. Greis—the neonatal trauma specialist— was standing by when a social worker came out to talk to Craig.

"Dr. Bowen is doing everything she can," she'd told him. "But you should know that she might not be able to save both your wife and your baby."

"Save Tess," he'd responded without hesitation.

Because in that moment, he'd finally realized the truth that had eluded him for so long: he loved her.

He knew Tess would be devastated if she lost this baby, and he would, too. But they might be able to have other babies someday, and even if they couldn't, at least they'd have each other.

But the thought of losing Tess—no, he couldn't let that happen.

The social worker had shaken her head sympathetically. "You don't get to choose, Mr. Richmond. If the doctor can get in and get the baby out in time, then his chances are good. But she won't know your wife's chances until the baby is delivered."

And now all Craig could do was wait.

He sank into one of the hard plastic chairs that lined the walls of the dreary room and pressed the heels of his hands to his eyes. She'd lost so much blood. Maybe too much. And if they didn't stop the bleeding, she could die.

She could actually die.

And if he lost her, Craig knew that something inside him would die, too.

He heard footsteps near the door and his head shot up. He blinked away the moisture that blurred his eyes, desperately hoping it was Dr. Bowen coming back or anyone else who could tell him what was going on with Tess.

But it was his mom and dad and though he was disappointed, he was also glad for their presence.

"How is she?" Grace's voice was soft, but he saw the same strain and worry on her face that were etched in his own.

This wasn't easy for any of them. He knew how

much his mother and father cared about Tess, how excited they were about their first grandchild and how scared they must be for both Tess and the baby right now.

Craig could only shake his head helplessly. "I don't know. They took her away as soon as we got here and no one's been able to tell me anything since then." His eyes locked on the double doors that led to the emergency room. "It seems like she's been in there forever."

"We've got some of the best doctors in the country at this hospital," his father said.

"I hate feeling so helpless," Craig admitted. "Knowing that her life is on the line and there's nothing I can do."

"You can pray," Grace said.

And he had been—steadily and fervently—since they'd brought Tess in. Although he'd never been a very religious person, he was begging God now, pleading with Him to save his wife and baby.

"Your brother's on his way," Grace said. "And I called Tess's sister. She's going to come, too, as soon as she can."

"Thank you," Craig said.

"In the meantime, I'm going to go to the chapel. Do you want to come with me?"

He shook his head. "I can't. I need to stay here...in case there's any news."

His mother nodded. "I won't be long."

Allan came back—Craig hadn't even realized he'd gone until he returned—and pressed a cup into Craig's hands.

"Thanks," Craig said automatically, although he made no effort to drink it.

His dad sank into the vacant chair beside him.

"She's strong," Allan said. "And she's worked too hard to do what was right for this baby to give up now."

He was right. Tess was strong. Strong and stubborn and sexy and kind and generous and loving. She was honest and beautiful and real.

And with Tess, Craig had found the fulfillment and contentment that had always seemed unattainable. With Tess, he didn't wonder about what he was missing out on, what was missing from his life because his life was finally complete. Because he'd finally been lucky enough to find a woman who really loved him and whom he could love back.

And he was going to tell her exactly that the first chance he got and every day for the rest of their lives together because he refused to believe that he'd finally found love only to have it taken away from him.

When Tess woke up she was in a hospital bed, Craig sitting in the chair beside her.

She had a moment of confusion, thinking she was still in San Diego, still months away from her due date. Then disjointed memories of the past several hours rushed through her mind and she slowly sorted through them. The contractions. The ambulance. Bits and pieces of conversation nudged at her consciousness. Emergency C-section. Severe blood loss. Shock. Fetal distress.

"The baby?" she asked.

"Right here." Craig shifted closer, and she finally noticed the tiny wrapped bundle cradled in his arms.

"Oh." She exhaled a shaky sigh as more memories

filtered through the haze and she remembered hearing the indignant cries of her baby as they pulled him out of her belly. It was the most beautiful sound she'd ever heard.

Craig laid the baby on the bed beside her. "Five pounds ten ounces, healthy and strong. You did a great job, Tess."

She felt the sting of happy tears as she gazed at her beautiful baby. "Wow."

He smiled. "That was my first reaction, too."

"It seems like we waited for him for so long and now he's finally here."

"Yeah. Except that he's a girl."

"A girl?" she echoed, certain she hadn't heard him correctly.

"They ran out of pink blankets—that's why she's in blue," he explained. "But she's very definitely a girl."

"Oh."

"You're not disappointed, are you?" Craig asked.

"Of course not. I'm just surprised."

"We're going to have to come up with another name," he told her.

They'd chosen Jacob Allan when they'd believed the baby was a boy but had never settled on a girl's name because they hadn't thought they'd need one.

"Grace Catherine Richmond," she said.

Grace for his mother, of course, and Catherine for hers.

She watched surprise flicker over his face, then pleasure. "I think it's perfect."

Tess touched her lips to the soft downy hair at the baby's temple. "Me, too."

"There's something else I need to tell you."

"There's not another baby," she said, remembering all the times he'd teased her about the possibility of twins. "The ultrasound technician might have made a mistake about the baby's gender, but she was very clear that there was only one baby."

"No, there's not another baby," he said, then grinned. "Not yet, anyway."

"Then what is it?"

"I love you, Tess."

She stared at him, certain she couldn't have heard him correctly. "What?"

"I probably should have set the scene," he said, almost to himself. "With flowers, soft music, candlelight. Not mint-green walls and the antiseptic smell of a hospital room. But after everything that's happened today, I didn't want to wait. The most important thing is that we're here together—you and me and our baby girl."

Then he leaned over to kiss her. It was a gentle brush of his lips on hers, fleeting and soft and infinitely sweet.

As much as she enjoyed the kiss, she wanted to hear him say the words again—if he'd, in fact, said them the first time and she wasn't having some kind of drug-induced hallucination.

But as he continued to kiss her, she remembered what Grace had said and she realized her mother-in-law was right. She'd been too hung up on wanting to hear the words that she'd missed seeing the proof of his love in all the little things he said and did. Like right now.

She sighed softly, contentedly as he eased his lips from hers.

"I really do love you, Tess."

And suddenly her heart felt as if it was going to burst right out of her chest.

"I know it took me a while to realize it but it's true and if you'll marry me—I'll spend the rest of my life proving it to you."

It was the longest explanation of his emotions he'd ever given and Craig had never been as nervous as he was in that moment, waiting for Tess to respond to his declaration.

When she finally did speak, it was only to say, "Did you just ask me to marry you?"

"Yes."

"But we're already married."

He should have known she would get caught up in the technicalities.

"I know," he said. "But you were pregnant when I asked you the first dozen times and I know you think that was the only reason I proposed. And maybe at the time it was. But I've been thinking about all the reasons I want you to be my wife now and—" he pulled out a folded page out of his pocket "—I made a list."

"You're kidding?"

"Nope." He unfolded the paper and handed it to her.

He'd written a title at the top: Reasons I Want You to Marry Me. Then there was an itemized list numbered one through twenty-five, each line reading simply "I love you."

She looked at the list, then at him and back at the page again. But she didn't say anything.

"I could have written a hundred pages with the same words," he told her, "and they still wouldn't begin to describe how much I really do love you, Tess. Maybe I'm the world's biggest idiot for taking so long to figure it out but now that I have, I know that I want to spend every day of the rest of my life proving it to you.

"And I want to marry you again—to renew our vows—just because we love each other."

Still she hesitated and he felt his hope begin to fade. Maybe this was a bad idea. Maybe he'd waited too long. Or maybe he was rushing this—considering that she'd just had a baby and was recovering from emergency surgery. Or maybe as he was realizing how much he loved her, she'd realized she didn't love him anymore.

"That is," he said, "if you still love me."

This time when she glanced up from the paper in her hand he saw the depth of emotion in her eyes.

"I didn't choose to fall in love with you," she reminded him. "And I couldn't choose to stop even if I wanted to. But my feelings haven't changed.

"Or maybe they have. Because I love you even more now than I did then. So if you really want to get married again my answer is definitely yes."

"I really want to get married again," he assured her. "Because I've finally realized how lucky I am to have you—and I'm never going to let you go."

Then he cupped her face in his palms and pressed his lips to hers in a kiss filled with hope and love and promises. A kiss that was interrupted by the indignant cry of a newborn baby who wanted her daddy to know he was going to have to share mommy's attention.

Craig reluctantly eased away to look down at their baby girl. "She's probably hungry."

"She must have worked up an appetite—it's hard work being born."

"She certainly didn't do it the easy way," Craig

agreed, watching as Tess unbuttoned her gown to put the baby to her breast.

Gracie rooted around for a moment before she found the nipple, but when she did, she latched right on and began to suckle. It was the most amazing thing Craig had ever seen—his beautiful wife nursing their beautiful daughter.

"I thought it would be harder than that," Tess murmured, stroking a finger gently over the soft, downy hair on top of Gracie's head.

"Some things are just natural," he told her.

And he knew now without a doubt that, for him, loving Tess was one of those things.

Epilogue

Tess lifted the flap of the envelope, pulled out two airline tickets. "What's this?"

"Your anniversary present," Craig said and smiled at her. "Two weeks in Barbados, just me and you."

"What about the kids?"

"Grandma and Grandpa Richmond are looking forward to having their house turned upside down by our rugrats."

"For two whole weeks?" Tess couldn't believe anyone would volunteer for such a momentous undertaking. Gracie was now nine and a half years old, the twins—Eryn and Allie—were almost seven and Lucy had just turned four. Of course, their grandparents thought they were all little angels. Well, two weeks under the same roof would certainly change *that* opinion.

"I thought we deserved to do something special for

our tenth anniversary." He slipped his arms around her waist and drew her closer. "Or is it only our ninth?"

"Both." They had renewed their vows, as Craig had wanted, on the first anniversary of their wedding.

"So, what do you think? Are you ready to ditch our kids for two weeks alone with me?"

After ten years, the passion between them had not dimmed and she was very much looking forward to the opportunity to spend some uninterrupted time with her husband. She tossed the tickets aside to link her hands behind her husband's neck. "Definitely."

"I love you, Tess."

And just like the first time he'd ever said those words to her, her heart expanded with so much joy she thought it might burst. "I love you, too."

"Remember all the sightseeing we did on our first honeymoon?" he asked.

"Yes."

He grinned lasciviously. "Good. Then we don't have to do all of that again."

"So what will we do for two whole weeks?"

"It will be my very great pleasure to show you," he whispered the words against her mouth before deepening the kiss.

She let her eyes drift shut, felt herself drowning in a myriad of sensations. Would she ever get used to the explosive currents that raced through her at his simplest touch?

She didn't think so, but they had the rest of their lives together to find out for sure.

* * * * *

Mills & Boon® Special Edition
brings you a sneak preview of Marie Ferrarella's
Capturing the Millionaire...

*It was a dark and stormy night...when lawyer
Alain Dulac crashed his BMW into a tree, and
local vet Kayla McKenna came to his aid. Used
to rescuing dogs and cats, Kayla didn't know
what to make of this stranger...but his
magnetism was undeniable...*

Don't miss the fantastic third story in
THE SONS OF LILY MOREAU *series,
available next month, October 2008, in
Mills & Boon® Special Edition!*

Capturing the Millionaire

by

Marie Ferrarella

The first thing Alain became aware of as he slowly pried his eyes opened, was the weight of the anvil currently residing on his forehead. It felt as if it weighed a thousand pounds, and a gaggle of devils danced along its surface, each taking a swing with his hammer as he passed.

The second thing he became aware of was the feel of the sheets against his skin. Against almost *all* of his skin. He was naked beneath the blue-and-white down comforter. Or close to it. He definitely felt linen beneath his shoulders.

Blinking, he tried very hard to focus his eyes.

Where the hell was he?

He had absolutely no idea how he had gotten here—or what he was doing here to begin with.

Or, for that matter, who that woman with the shapely hips was.

Alain blinked again. He wasn't imagining it. There was a woman with her back to him, a woman with sumptuous hips, bending over a fireplace. The glow from the hearth, and a handful of candles scattered throughout the large, rustic-looking room provided the only light to be had.

Why? Where was the electricity? Had he crossed some time warp?

Nothing was making any sense. Alain tried to raise his head, and instantly regretted it. The pounding intensified twofold.

His hand automatically flew to his forehead and came in contact with a sea of gauze. He slowly moved his fingertips along it.

What had happened?

Curious, he raised the comforter and sheet and saw he still had on his briefs. There were more bandages, these wrapped tightly around his chest. He was beginning to feel like some sort of cartoon character.

Alain opened his mouth to get the woman's attention, but nothing came out. He cleared his throat before making another attempt, and she heard him.

She turned around—as did the pack of dogs that were gathered around her. Alain realized that she'd been putting food into their bowls.

Good, at least they weren't going to eat him.

Yet, he amended warily.

"You're awake," she said, looking pleased as she crossed over to him. The light from the fireplace caught in the swirls of red hair that framed her face. She moved fluidly, with grace. Like someone who was comfortable within her own skin. And why not? The woman was beautiful.

Again, he wondered if he was dreaming.

"And naked," he added.

A rueful smile slipped across her lips. He couldn't tell if it was light from the fire or if a pink hue had just crept up her cheeks. In any event, it was alluring.

"Sorry about that."

"Why, did you have your way with me?" he asked, a hint of amusement winning out over his confusion.

"You're not naked," she pointed out. "And I prefer my men to be conscious." Then she became serious. "Your clothes were all muddy and wet. I managed to wash them before the power went out completely." She gestured about the room, toward the many candles set on half the flat surfaces. "They're hanging in my garage right now, but they're not going to be dry until morning," she said apologetically. "If then."

He was familiar with power outages; they usually lasted only a few minutes. "Unless the power comes back on."

The redhead shook her head, her hair moving about her face like an airy cloud. "Highly doubtful. When we lose power around here, it's hardly ever a short-term thing. If we're lucky, we'll get power back by midafternoon tomorrow."

Alain glanced down at the coverlet spread over his body. Even that slight movement hurt his neck. "Well, as intriguing as the whole idea might be, I really can't stay naked all that time. Can I borrow some clothes from your husband until mine are ready?"

Was that amusement in her eyes, or something else? "That might not be so easy," she told him.

"Why?"

"Because I don't have one."

He'd thought he'd seen someone in a hooded rain slicker earlier. "Significant other?" he suggested. When she made no response, he continued, "Brother? Father?"

She shook her head at each suggestion. "None of the above."

"You're alone?" he questioned incredulously.

"I currently have seven dogs," she told him, amusement playing along her lips. "Never, at any time of the night or day, am I alone."

He didn't understand. If there was no other person in the house—

"Then how did you get me in here? You sure as hell don't look strong enough to have carried me all the way by yourself."

She pointed toward the oilcloth she'd left spread out and drying before the fireplace. "I put you in that and dragged you in."

He had to admit he was impressed. None of the women he'd ever met would have even attempted to do anything like that. They would likely have left him out in the rain until he was capable of moving on his own power. Or drowned.

"Resourceful."

"I like to think so." And, being resourceful, her mind was never still. It now attacked the problem of the all-but-naked man in her living room. "You know, I think there might be a pair of my dad's old coveralls in the attic." As she talked, Kayla started to make her way toward the stairs, and then stopped. A skeptical expression entered her bright-green eyes as they swept over the man on the sofa.

Alain saw the look and couldn't help wondering what she was thinking. Why was there a doubtful frown on her face? "What?"

"Well…" Kayla hesitated, searching for a delicate way to phrase this, even though her father had been gone for some five years now. "My dad was a pretty big man."

Alain still didn't see what the problem was. "I'm six-two."

She smiled, and despite the situation, he found himself being drawn in as surely as if someone had thrown a rope over him and begun to pull him closer.

"No, not big—" Kayla held her hand up to indicate height "—big." This time, she moved her hand in front of her, about chest level, to denote a man whose build had been once compared to that of an overgrown grizzly bear.

"I'll take my chances," Alain assured her. "It's either that or wear something of yours, and I don't think either one of us wants to go that route."

It suddenly occurred to him that he was having a conversation with a woman whose name he didn't know and who didn't know his. While that was not an entirely unusual situation for him, an introduction was definitely due.

"By the way, I'm Alain Dulac."

Her smile, he thought, seemed to light up the room far better than the candles did.

"Kayla," she told him. "Kayla McKenna."

* * * * *

Don't forget Capturing the Millionaire *is available in October 2008.*

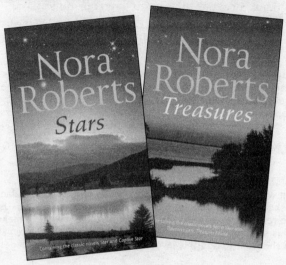

FREE!

4 Books
and a surprise gift!

We would like to take this opportunity to thank you for reading this Mills & Boon® book by offering you the chance to take FOUR more specially selected titles from the Special Edition series absolutely FREE! We're also making this offer to introduce you to the benefits of the Mills & Boon® Book Club—

- ★ **FREE home delivery**
- ★ **FREE gifts and competitions**
- ★ **FREE monthly Newsletter**
- ★ **Exclusive Mills & Boon Book Club offers**
- ★ **Books available before they're in the shops**

Accepting these FREE books and gift places you under no obligation to buy, you may cancel at any time, even after receiving your free shipment. Simply complete your details below and return the entire page to the address below. You don't even need a stamp!

YES! Please send me 4 free Special Edition books and a surprise gift. I understand that unless you hear from me, I will receive 6 superb new titles every month for just £3.15 each, postage and packing free. I am under no obligation to purchase any books and may cancel my subscription at any time. The free books and gift will be mine to keep in any case.

E8ZEF

Ms/Mrs/Miss/Mr ....Initials ....
BLOCK CAPITALS PLEASE

Surname ....

Address ....

....

....Postcode ....

Send this whole page to:
UK: FREEPOST CN81, Croydon, CR9 3WZ